A PARALLEL LIFE

A
Parallel
Life

Lorraine White

UNITED WRITERS
Cornwall

UNITED WRITERS PUBLICATIONS LTD
Ailsa, Castle Gate, Penzance, Cornwall.
www.unitedwriters.co.uk

British Library Cataloguing in Publication Data:
A catalogue record for this book is
available from the British Library.

ISBN 9781852001940

Printed and bound in Great Britain by
United Writers Publications Ltd.,
Cornwall.

For Michael,
Christopher and Hannah.
With love.

Acknowledgements

I would like to say a huge thank you to my family for their support: my husband, Michael; my son, Christopher; and my daughter, Hannah. They have all been amazingly enthusiastic about this whole venture.

Without readers, of course, there would be little point to any of this other than the personal enjoyment of writing. I am truly grateful to anyone who takes the time to read this novel.

Huge thanks must also go to Malcolm Sheppard and his team. They saw the potential in my work and assisted me during every step of this journey to 'A Parallel Life'.

Contents

Page

The Chapters in Myra's Book of Life

1 Reality: The Inspiration — 11

Part One – Fiction: The Future World — 19

2 Reality: Initial Thoughts — 27

Part Two – Fiction: The Beginning — 29

3 Reality: A New Idea — 42

Part Three – Fiction: 2323: The Present — 46

4 Reality: Alone — 56

Part Four – Fiction: The Final Days of Childhood — 60

5 Reality: A Fortuitous Spillage — 85

Part Five – Fiction: Lisa Watts — 87

6 Reality: A walk in the Park — 96

Part Six – Fiction: Outside The Wall — 99

7 Reality: Howie Redman — 108

Part Seven – Fiction: Rusty — 110

8 Reality: A Good Idea — 114

Part Eight – Fiction: May Kilman — 116

9 Reality: April 2018 — 119

Part Nine – Fiction: Unexpectedly Alive — 130

10 Reality: Old Tricks — 137

Part Ten – Fiction: The Denouement — 140

11 Reality: Myra's de die in diem — 152

The Chapters in Anita's Book of Life

1 Reality: Thinking about the Past:
   Trying to Establish the Motivation — 191

2 Reality: Thinking about the Future:
   Fulfilling Myra's Vision — 194

The Chapters in Myra's Book of Life

Reality

Chapter One

The Inspiration

2002: The Past.

Both Arthur Vilas and his nine year old daughter had become sadly accustomed to the uniformity of the interminable beep emanating from the life support machine. They sat in silence on either side of the woman who lay in a critical condition on the bed between them as she slowly approached death: a woman who had once possessed such vigour, such vivacity. At no time did the daughter look towards her father; her steadfast gaze was focused entirely on the face of the recumbent woman. The eyes of the father flitted apprehensively from hand, to wife, to daughter as he nervously twisted his wedding ring round and round and round on his finger.

Neither of them was truly prepared for the sudden jolt as the steady beat that had lulled them into a fragile sense of security became an insistent unremitting distress alarm.

Myra screamed, jumping up in her hysteria and desperately shaking the inert body in front of her, "You can't die! You can't die!"

Mr Vilas had also risen at this point, reaching across the bed in an attempt to intervene as nurses and doctors rushed into the hospital room.

"Get your daughter out of here," came the quiet but very firmly spoken instruction.

Vilas hurried around the bed towards his daughter, but before he got to her she turned and screamed again; this time it wasn't a scream of despair, it was a scream of pure venom. This time her words were clearly aimed directly at him, "Don't touch me. Don't you dare touch me! This is your fault. This is all your fault!"

A nurse, pushing her way past the father, grabbed the girl's arm, pulling her forward towards the door and then, meeting with unprecedented resistance, dragged her firmly out of the room. She forced the bawling child into a nearby consultancy office and sat her down, turning towards the helpless father as he hovered in their wake. "I suggest, under the circumstances, that you take a seat in the corridor outside, Mr Vilas. I will deal with this child. My colleagues will do all they can for your wife."

Inside the consultancy room, with the help of the nurse, the volcanic eruption that was Myra gradually calmed to become a bubbling cauldron as the young girl started to take control of her emotions. The nurse spoke reassuring words while Arthur Vilas sat out in the corridor anxiously waiting for someone to tell him what was going on.

The child looked through the window that separated the room from the corridor outside. A doctor approached. Her father stood up. The doctor spoke: unheard words. Arthur Vilas' whole body crumpled as he collapsed onto the bench: uncontrollable shaking overpowered his entire being. His world had fallen apart.

Myra knew that the woman, her mother, who lay on the bed in the next room, was gone. Mrs Celia Vilas ceased to exist.

The frantic activity of the medical staff ground to a halt and all of them slowly and automatically went about their duties, each in the full knowledge of his or her individual responsibility. The unfortunate death of one patient did not stop the workings of the whole establishment however deeply they felt about it. They had done all they could and now they had to attend to other priorities; as did Arthur Vilas and his daughter Myra Vilas, who had their lives alone together stretching before them.

2018: Sixteen Years Later. The Present.

Myra's visit to the nearby church had been somewhat unsatisfactory, although in all honesty a fairly predictable outcome to a failed impracticable pipe dream. It had been a last futile hope that a miracle would occur, that a vision would appear which could help guide her towards a resolution and possibly a new approach to life. In short: a future.

She had recently read a psychiatrist's article in a medical journal where the writer had suggested that the importance of religion, or lack of it, has a large part to play in a young adult's feeling of worth. He purported that a significant feature of religious belief is the value that is placed on the intrinsic rather than on material wealth. Indeed, Myra did confess that an unwavering confidence in God had given her own grandparents a lifelong purpose. She had personally never really understood the appeal. For her generation, worldly possessions and image, not prayer, had become the personal lifelong project.

By finally deciding to visit the nearby church and attempting, albeit rather too briefly, to embrace its ambience, Myra had vainly hoped to find some answers to what might be the fundamental cause of her insecurities. Despite her hopes, she had left sadly disappointed and somewhat disillusioned by the experience. It is, however, extremely difficult if not impossible to find answers when you are not entirely sure what the questions are.

What she felt now, though, was anger: an anger that was rooted in her own vulnerability and yet, typical of her approach to life, she was unprepared to blame herself or her own weaknesses for this instinctive reaction. On this particular day she blamed religion; it was blatantly obvious to her that religious faith was a fool's paradise. She was now more convinced than ever that a church was just a building. Nothing more. Nothing less. And yet it was a very self-indulgent and austere building which had been able to con her with an inexplicable magnetism that had pulled her into its bowels to view its jealously guarded precious inner treasures. Inner treasures which ultimately proved to be material and not intrinsic. As she walked down the aisles, she could almost hear the sibilant voice of Tolkien's Gollum pervading the nave with its whispers of "My precious".

And what treasures there were! Masterpieces adorned the walls; statues stood proudly in every conceivable niche; silver candleholders, like sentinels, guarded the front altar in its sanctuary. There was the ornate golden eagle lectern on whose outstretched wings rested the bible: a book of pure fiction as far as she was concerned.

Then there was the altar itself: a table, just a table, but a table that seemed to hold such significance for so many people. Stretched across it, having undoubtedly been placed there with immense care by some elderly devotee, was a beautifully embroidered altar cloth. Not a single crease spoilt the pristine effect. Someone had clearly spent many arduous hours embellishing this length of material. Why?

And behind that table, was a huge crucifix. She looked up half expecting a tear to gradually trickle down from the sad eyes of Jesus, but this wasn't a movie set or a Madonna video, this was real life. She turned to leave.

What faced her was an empty church with row upon row of hardwood pews. The last time she had sat on one of those long, highly uncomfortable benches was sixteen years ago at her mother's funeral, surrounded by strangers. She had sat there, seemingly devoid of any emotion to all outward appearances, yet the inner turmoil was almost unbearable. She was totally unable to associate that bare wooden box with the effervescent woman who had always been there for her: a woman whose love for her daughter was entirely unconditional. Her mother had never been a particularly tactile parent or a person who openly professed her love but their relationship was unbreakable, or so Myra had thought. How could a nine year old girl explain how she felt? There was anger, confusion, guilt and a deep-seated anguish in the pit of her stomach. Responsibility had to be taken for her mother's untimely death and justice was imperative.

And now, sixteen years later, she had finally found the courage to visit this hallowed place only to feel cheated. This cold building had nothing to offer her: no loving memory of her mother; no comfort for her loss. There was nothing here to alleviate the pain of that day: the day she had to say goodbye to her beloved mamma.

Myra privately conceded that throughout her life she had always been a difficult person to satisfy. As she walked back to her awaiting apartment she could not help but feel a small touch of guilt at the thought of what she considered to be the only redeeming feature for her regarding the visit. It was the youthful beauty of the verger whose footsteps echoed around the building as he walked down the central aisle to speak with this young mother who had come in from the cold to visit the church. What a waste! She smiled to herself as she thought about his deep green eyes, his infectious welcoming smile and his subsequent look of consternation as she questioned the unnecessary wealth of the church and its doubtful role in modern society. Perhaps it was not a good idea to place the poor young man, having not long left boyhood himself, in such a difficult position as to openly flirt with him, a man of the cloth, especially while she was pushing a tiny baby in a buggy.

He kindly helped her with the huge, studded door when she left. On looking back after manoeuvring the buggy onto the tarmacadam path, she noticed that the portal had been closed before she even had the chance to thank him: the young man had escaped as quickly as he could. He had found the sanctuary he desired! She imagined his relief.

Back at the apartment, she lifted Miriam slightly clumsily from the buggy. Holding her small child at arms' length, she looked into those as yet uncorrupted, bright blue eyes. "Well Miriam. What am I to do? I can't ask you for advice, can I?"

The little bundle gurgled happily in response, unaccustomed to this intimate attention from her mother. Myra put her on the floor and sat by her side. "I'm twenty-five. I'm healthy. I have all the money I need. I'm attractive. I have a fabulous apartment and yet, my wriggling little jewel, I am lost. I am a modern success story, so why am I not happy?" She sighed. A deep heavy sigh.

"I am certainly not where I thought I would be at this age. The church clearly has nothing to offer me; that's blatantly obvious. And I don't believe that Social Services have anything to offer me. My very busy doctor, who has got better things to do with his time than listen to the ramblings of a rich, upwardly mobile twenty-something of the modern era, has nothing to offer me. Apparently, I can receive counselling. I could be referred to, and I quote, 'Stay in a safe environment that calms me down sufficiently so that my relationship with the real world can be forged again.' What good would that do? Where is safer than here in my own apartment? Isn't this the real world?

"Oh, and of course there is my family of one, my father, your grandfather. He definitely has nothing to offer me: apart from money.

"And before you say anything, my little precious, I do not want a husband; one self-important male trying to dominate my life is never going to satisfy all of my needs! Marriage is not part of my ideal lifestyle. Did you know that two in five marriages in this country end in divorce? Anyway, I have only ever loved one person and, regrettably, there is no way that marriage is an option there.

"Well, you know what I am going to do? It might sound ridiculous to you but I am going to write. I'm going to immerse myself in the written word. I'm going to write and write and write in my own inimitable fashion."

She paused and her eyes became lost in the past. The baby at her feet quietly watched her mother.

"Do you remember when I was apparently suffering from an eating disorder, it was suggested that I write a diary to get my thoughts out into the open? And yet I was given the option to keep the diary private. How is that getting my thoughts out into the open? Anyway, of course you don't remember; you weren't even born. As much as I hate to admit it, that diary helped. A simple process, admittedly, but I realised that I actually enjoy writing; I can put on paper things I can't say to people. I can let my emotions flow on to the blank page and nobody realises the poignancy behind the words. Nobody knows who I truly am. I can hide behind the persona. The catharsis is liberating – whoops, sorry little one, these words are probably a bit too long for you.

"Anyway, Miriam, I started a career, if that's what you can call it. I wrote novels. There was a change of name here and there; a change of venue; an added bit of violence for effect. I can't really say that I am the most successful novelist in the world. Your grandfather's money certainly comes in handy." She lifted up her young daughter.

"Do you know what? I am going to do that again. I think that I have been waiting for a long time to write this and now I'm ready. A diary. A fictional parallel to the life of Myra Vilas: the human conundrum.

"The world might not be ready, but I am."

Myra removed Miriam's outdoor wear and took the child into her room. There was no nappy check. There was no eye contact. She placed the small human bundle in to her cot surrounded by all manner of toys and playthings to keep her amused. The baby

16

whimpered in futile protest; she had enjoyed the comforting voice of her mother, but she soon became fascinated by the twirling animals flying above her and the softness of the cuddlies against her skin.

Thus the time had finally arrived for Myra to start the manuscript: the most important piece of her writing career thus far. It would be her tour de force. It would not be a diary as such. It might be a novel; it might be a novella, more compact in its approach. She had not as yet decided, but what she did know was that she had something very important to say and this would be her method: her pathway to closure. Her catharsis.

As the author of her own novel, there was no disputing the fact that she had full control over every word that was written: her omnipotence was irrefutable. Did this mean, however, that she would be tempted to manipulate the final outcome? And, if she did this, surely the very act of deliberate modification would mean that she could never achieve complete reparation for past wrongs?

In her day to day existence she had often heard the phrase, 'At least you tried.' But she wanted to do more than just try. Did people really believe that exoneration was feasible just by attempting something and that previous transgression could be forgotten? Could the mere act of writing redress the balance and fully compensate for all that had happened? The attempt alone was not everything. She wanted to succeed and she truly believed that a person must not merely attempt; a person must achieve. If a particular approach did not work, then another approach must be found.

In her teenage years, Myra's mantra had always been to make it a rule of life never to regret anything and never to look back, but she did not feel that she had been totally successful in this strategy. In her heart of hearts, she didn't fully believe in this philosophy. Regret was indeed a negative emotional state that had a tendency to pop up unannounced and unwanted, but it could be a useful tool. Surely regret could be a helpful emotion during the maturing process? Never looking back should never be an option in any human being's life. The pain of regret could help someone to refocus, take corrective action and pursue a new path. This, finally, is what she intended to do.

17

Despite her outward appearance to all who knew her as that of a highly confident young lady, an underlying uncertainty had haunted her for a number of years; further attacking her resolve. But now was the time; she was ready and she would succeed. She did not consider herself as some omniscient being, but she did have absolute power, not only over the outcome of the novel but also over the outcome of her life beyond the novel. Her manuscript, albeit ostensibly fictional, would be a revelation: a stepping stone towards her personal indemnity. Any subsequent actions would be justified and atonement would be fulfilled; if indeed it was atonement that she was seeking.

She looked down at her notebook and pulled back its stiff front cover to reveal the opening page and its colour of innocence. It was as yet unsullied by any useful jottings needed to help in the preparation for her final project. The binding of the notebook was a little resistant but this newness would soon disappear. She would take the book everywhere with her: her constant companion. Its simple messages would become her aide-memoire before she embarked upon the manuscript itself. Happy with her note making, she could then fill the computer's blank screen to create her story.

Deep in her heart she knew that she would never reach the heady heights of an internationally famous author. She believed herself to be a reasonably proficient writer but not a great writer. Nor would she ever be. She had received many rejections from a variety of publishers; she was not particularly comfortable with the idea of self-publishing so she had never pursued that channel. But this was a pivotal moment in her life and Myra Vilas had a critical message to give and, if necessary, critical subsequent action to be taken.

She put pen to paper. In vain, the binding of the notebook creaked its resistance. She had begun; control would be restored.

Myra's manuscript notes:

Passing of time
Future consequences
A future world: context. NO religion!
Family life
Male vs female

*"We are faced with a myriad of possible futures;
this is only one of them."* Myra Vilas.

Fiction

The Manuscript
Part One

The Future World

The Lead up to the Twenty-fourth Century
*On June 10th 2013, the BBC Radio 4 news announced that in
certain areas of the country's main cities, 65% of households had
no father figure. There were children and mothers, but no fathers;
there was no male role model.*

*Concerns were voiced by postulatory experts that children no
longer had "meaningful contact with their fathers" and this
would inevitably lead to "teenage pregnancy, crime and
disadvantage". There were fears that 'men deserts' would be
strewn across the country and, of course, consideration needed to
be given to the financial pressures on society, "Family breakdown
costs us fifty billion pounds a year" stated one so-called expert,
who went on to say that these pockets of single mothers, "lead to
poverty".*

*As the years went by, similar 'men deserts' did start to spring
up across the country. Something had to be done. And it was.
Contrary to the experts' predictions, teenage pregnancy figures
did not rise; crime did not rise. However, it could certainly be
argued that disadvantage did rise. But was the disadvantage of
which these experts talked, the disadvantage that actually
occurred?*

*By the time humanity reached the twenty-fourth century, over
three hundred years later, all towns and cities in society were*

enclosed within high, insurmountable walls and on each lay an immense domed roof. In certain circumstances, the roof could be opened exposing the township to the world beyond and allowing unmanned service aircraft to visit other areas. On these particular occasions, wailing sirens heralded a deadly warning and automated megaphones instructed all citizens to stay inside. Being subjected to the alien and dangerous atmosphere beyond the limits of any township would result in poisoning, ultimately leading to an agonising death.

The citizens themselves were not permitted to leave their towns or cities; no communication whatsoever was permitted between the general populace of any settlement. Holidays in other townships or areas were unheard of. Holidays were unheard of.

The thick grey walls that surrounded the townships seemed to reach endlessly skyward. They were made from a reinforced composite of metal and stone making a totally impenetrable barrier between the townships and the world beyond. The world beyond was a wild, untameable wilderness, comprising an atmosphere that could not be survived by humans: or so people were led to believe. The general populace were, indeed, led to believe many spurious aspects of their society and only a minority of people fully comprehended that governmental information could not always be relied upon.

No religious buildings existed within the townships. Chapels, churches, cathedrals, synagogues, mosques: all places of worship were destroyed during the late twenty-second and early twenty-third centuries. Religion was, of course, the root of all conflict and the root of all conflict should be removed. For many years, religion had allowed the exploitation of vulnerable people; the religious hierarchy had turned a blind eye to heinous acts against young citizens. And it was widely understood, of course, that religion was the motivation behind every global war.

All silverware and any other precious metal within these religious buildings was melted down to be used for more practical purposes, such as dental alloys, solder and brazing alloys, electrical contacts and batteries. Everything was used to further the technological advances one would expect during the twenty-fourth century.

Technological advances were certainly in evidence but what about societal advances? What about people's freedom? Any places that encouraged groups to meet in order to socialise; to worship; to have any common interests; were seen as an opportunity to plot against the ruling authority and were, therefore, unlawful. And it was the use of technological advances that contributed towards this loss of freedom. Androids, drones, computers: all were employed to stifle people's liberty. These machines were for governmental forces' use only; the general public were not permitted to take advantage of any of these technological advances.

With regard to entertainment, all citizens were permitted to listen to live music or musical recordings transmitted on radios. These radios had only one channel; it was accessible to the Government and scrutinised accordingly. The music had to be instrumental only, thus eliminating the possibility of sending the general populace any undesirable or clandestine verbal messages. There were large venue halls that people could visit and attend concerts. Every member of the audience was thoroughly searched prior to entering the venue. The auditorium remained fully lit throughout the performance in order that the audience could be observed with the use of spy cameras.

All of the music to be performed at the concert was vetted in advance. It was not unusual for an evening's entertainment to be cancelled at the last minute due to an unknown authoritarian governmental representative taking a dislike to the music that was going to be performed. This could, on occasions, lead to the arrest of the musicians. Being a musician was a precarious occupation that very few people were willing to undertake. Programmable androids were beginning to monopolise this profession which resulted in smaller audiences; many felt that the machines did not have an innate feel for the music to be performed. How could a machine embrace the heart and soul of a musical composition?

With regard to personal appearance, no citizen was permitted to wear jewellery that signified membership of a sect or club: religious icons were certainly an anathema. In fact, the wearing of any jewellery, although not unlawful, was heralded as being pretentious and, as such, was not encouraged. Any individual who was coupled to another was permitted to wear a simple band of gold, silver or platinum on the third finger of the left hand: a tradition that had been in evidence for many years. Excess *jewellery was perceived as frivolous, as was the wearing of brightly coloured clothing. Neither of these was as yet illegal, but was clearly viewed with contempt.*

The air temperature within the townships was strictly controlled, eliminating natural rain and snow but allowing an occasional moist breeze to ensure a healthy atmosphere. That is not to say that the temperature remained constant; it did not. There were hot days, really hot days, cold days, really cold days; just enough unpredictability to keep people alert; just a small measure to ensure that people did not become too complacent. Artificial rain, hail and snow occasionally formed an intrinsic part of this manmade weather system. A corporate decision had also been made to maintain, through use of artificial lighting, the concept of night and day.

There were no animals. Squads of government employees patrolled all areas with the sole purpose of eliminating any living creatures other than, of course, the resident human inhabitants. Most of the people had never seen a dog, a rat, a cat or even any type of insect that early ancestors might have felt had plagued the lives of the twenty-first century human. The inherent air conditioning present in all buildings maintained an influx of insecticide which helped to eradicate any errant wasp, ant or daddy-long-legs, but was harmless to humans. However, some suspected that it also made people feel lethargic, and therefore more submissive and compliant. The keeping of domesticated pets had long since been abolished; children would probably have screamed at the sight of a hamster or gerbil.

Every walled township and city within the country was further divided into three clearly demarcated sectors: Female Sectors, Male Sectors and Couple Sectors. There was a fourth sector, far less highly regarded by those in authority who were unhappy with what might be considered as dubiety in the structure of the community: the Transient Sector. If there were any disputes regarding residency in any of the sectors, a session was held by the Governmental Court of Residency and their decision was final. The Transient Sector was where people stayed whose cases were being considered, and thus, was less comfortable for the residents. This inherent lack of comfort supposedly encouraged the temporary nature of the residency. Long, grey, featureless corridors branched out to form diminutive, grey, featureless apartments. Unfortunately, the Transient Sector domicile had the potential for some citizens to become permanent: there was simply nowhere else to go.

In the Female Sectors, whole sections of cities and townships housed single mothers. Initially, men roamed freely around these streets. None actually lived there but with the passing of time and the domination of the ruling Official Government and its parochial policies, few men chose to pass through these areas, preferring to stay in their own sectors.

In these Female Sectors, the children lived with their mothers, not always even knowing the identity of their fathers. When children reached the age of twelve, boys were taken away, never to return to live with their mothers. They moved into the Male Sector; of course they could visit their mothers, but they could not live with them. At this age, both girls and boys sat a critical test, known as The Elevation Examination. As a result of this examination, some boys were employed by the township's Special Service; others were given menial jobs to perform for the 'good of society' such as being involved in the eradication of any roaming animals that may have ventured into the community from outside of The Wall or just helping to ensure that the streets remained litter-free. Those who joined the Special Service were seen to have the potential to further their career within the Government. They were graded as to their possible career path and they were given the appropriate training: they might be seen as having the potential to work in posts that required practical skills such as engineering; or their skills might be more suited to administrative tasks and they would be employed in one of the many offices within the walls of the Government buildings.

In contrast to this, following their test, the girls whose Elevation Examination results proved to be 'normal' – in other words acceptable in the eyes of the authorities – would be moved to another area of the Female Sector. They would have learned from their mothers the appropriate household skills and servitude and would eventually become mothers themselves. Those who were not placed in another area of the Female Sector were never seen again; these were the girls who scored too highly in The Elevation Examination. These were the girls who showed signs of possessing too high an intelligence quotient; they had the mental capacity and attitude to become Elevationists. Female

23

Elevationists were potentially too dangerous to society and needed to be eliminated; they might become overly confident in their own abilities to question or indeed change the very fabric of society, or they might have the potential to influence others to feel empowered to do likewise. Fear about these girls was said to have arisen from the growth of the feminist movement which for many citizens became an unfettered force during the mid to late twenty-first century. Although altruistic in its aims to establish educational and professional opportunities for women that could be perceived as being equal to those for men, inherent fears were such that men and even a number of women worked relentlessly to quash the movement.

Why were they afraid? It was, as is often the case, a fear totally founded upon lack of understanding. People believed that feminists wanted to control the world and put men down. Many feared that feminism would overturn time-honoured traditions, religious beliefs and established gender roles; the irony here, of course, was that with the quashing of the feminist movement there came the quashing of time-honoured traditions and religious beliefs, perhaps not, however, established gender roles. There had also been a concern that feminism would bring about negative shifts in relationships, marriage, society and culture. Most frightening of all was that feminism was associated with strong, forceful and angry women and this was just not acceptable. No woman had the right to elevate herself above any other man or woman.

And thus, a second specious fallacy was formulated and indeed encouraged by Governmental bodies in the twenty-fourth century cities and townships: young girls who proved to be potential Elevationists were actually taken away and put to death. There was some disagreement as to how this was accomplished; a lethal injection seemed to be the most popular conclusion, but others believed that girls were cremated, suffocated, put in a poisoned gas chamber or even hanged. This thought alone was enough to deter many mothers from trying to educate their young daughters, and so the male domination that had been an inherent aspect of human society for the millennia could continue.

In reality, the girls were transported to other cities and townships to be trained to work in their Government Offices. It was the potential for familial and sentimental influences from mothers that the Government felt needed to be eliminated, not the lives of the girls themselves. Nothing was done, however, to counter any rumours to the contrary. Without their mothers, the young girls could be moulded into having the correct attitude to focus on their work without distraction. In short, they could be indoctrinated.

The whole system was totally and utterly unfair. It clearly favoured able boys at the age of twelve, with no regard for their growing maturity or intellectual development beyond that age. It clearly did not favour girls in any way whatsoever. By no means were the majority of young citizens afforded the opportunity to reach their full potential. The result of the Elevation Examination was binding and irreversible.

It was not the case that women did not work within the Government Sector, but they rarely had the opportunity to further their career to become influential in any significant way. Any potential seen within a female to reach an elevated position in society was quashed without mercy. There was no Margaret Thatcher or Theresa May in 2323 and following the debacle of Queen Elizabeth's descendants during the late twenty-first century, the sovereign establishment fell into disrepute resulting in the royal dynasty coming to an end during the late twenty-second century. By 2300, the royal family no longer existed.

Only a few older women seemed to have some recollection of the joys of family life: a father, a mother and their children having meals together, going on holiday together, talking together. Or perhaps they thought they remembered; perhaps these were stories passed down from generation to generation of a past that possibly never existed. No women ever spoke of these memories in public and few ventured any comment even in the 'privacy' of their own homes. No one believed that such privacy existed.

Occasionally, a man and a woman lived together in a more luxurious sector of the city or township. But there were no children. Nor were there ever going to be. These areas were known as Couple Sectors. The women were barren. If the 'unmentionable' ever happened, the woman mysteriously disappeared for a short holiday during which time any unborn child was terminated. This was in the woman's best interests, as otherwise she would lose her status in the Couple Sector and

25

b

would probably not be seen there again, or at least not until her child had reached the age of twelve.

Male Sectors housed single men. These were the only areas where the crime figures fluctuated and armed Special Service Patrols became more and more evident in the streets.

The opportunity for men and women to meet naturally and fall in love began to diminish. Mobile phones and other electronic means of communication were strictly monitored. The citizens of the cities and townships were not allowed any such devices; landline telephones were permissible yet all knew that they were bugged by the authorities. Advanced electronic devices were only for use by Special Service Patrols and Government Agencies. The elimination of such devices for use by the general populace ensured that there was greater control over their activities. A dystopian society of the future had been created.

Reality

Chapter Two

Initial Thoughts

Myra looked at the screen and slowly scrolled down the pages, carefully reading through what she had typed out. She was reasonably happy with the vision of the future that she had created. It was not quite what she had originally intended but she had made a start. Well established writers might drip feed ideas about the structure of a society into their novel writing as it progressed, but she wanted to set the scene and then concentrate on the personalities within that background setting. It was the people that mattered to her; not the setting.

She conceded that she had possibly allowed her feminist views to influence her idea of the future in a rather dramatic way: unfortunately she could not help but be truly cynical about that future and what it held for women. Life had always been unfair and would undoubtedly always remain so. In the memorable allegorical words of George Orwell:

'ALL ANIMALS ARE EQUAL
BUT SOME ANIMALS ARE MORE EQUAL
THAN OTHERS.'

Now she could concentrate on the introduction of her 'animals' and their individual motivations. The year 2002, the pivotal point of her own life, was in the forefront of her mind, colouring her perception of her characters from the future.

Myra's manuscript notes:

Hospital and DEATH
Male domination
Male brutality

Fiction

The Manuscript
Part Two

The Beginning

January 2305: The Future Past

Both Nina and her husband were absolutely delighted when their closest of friends, Alice Silva, had asked them around for lunch at her luxurious apartment one Sunday in January. Alice was wife to Raymond Silva, the Head of Government and Societal Communication.

Hand in hand, Nina and Will walked tentatively in the icy weather: a short journey they had made many times before to visit their neighbours who lived only two apartment blocks away in the Couples Sector. Why the Government felt obliged to provide biting winds and freezing temperatures just to show some superfluous meteorological variation was beyond their understanding. Apparently the idea originated from a time when in some long forgotten era there was a natural demarcation of weather that was characterised by four separate seasons: winter, spring, summer and autumn. It was believed that January fell within the season known as winter: a time when the temperatures dropped and there was a high probability of precipitation of some sort on a daily basis.

Alice had clearly been looking out for them: the door was flung open before either of them had had a chance to let her know of their arrival. "Come in. Come in. Come in. I have such exciting news." She led them into her living area where a bottle of wine, undoubtedly of superior quality, and three crystal glasses were waiting on the table.

Will was the first to realise the significance of three rather than four glasses. "No Ray here today?"

"I can't wait for Raymond to come home. He's been called into work. I just want you both to be the first to hear our wonderful news." The next comment was made rather loudly as if some evident justification was necessary. "He knows you're coming round."

Then she smiled at them both, took a deep breath and announced, "We're going to have a child. I'm ten weeks pregnant."

A waterfall of thoughts cascaded into the minds of both visitors, but this time it was Nina who spoke first. "Congratulations. We're really pleased for you. That's fantastic news." The trite comments came one after another.

"We must have a drink to celebrate. Sit down both of you and I'll pour. It might have to be the last taste of alcohol I get for a while." She gave a nervous laugh. Alcoholic drinks were stringently rationed but it would seem that the rationing experienced by the majority of Lithport's citizens did not apply to Alice and Raymond Silva.

Nina ventured the next thought that was clearly in all of their minds. "You intend to keep the baby? You know the significance of that decision, Alice."

"Oh yes. There will be a few things to sort out but we'll manage. I am fully prepared to live in the Transient Sector on a temporary basis with Ray until an apartment can be found befitting the status of one of the highest ranking Government Officials. I am sure this will happen, but should that not be the case, I can live in the Female Sector and Ray can obtain an Official Pass allowing him to spend long periods of time with us: me and our new baby." This had all the characteristics of a prepared speech. She looked at them both and, with a depth of seriousness in her tone of voice that neither of them had ever heard before, she added, "I have no intention of terminating the pregnancy, and Raymond is just as determined; he has always wanted a child. Society needs to cater for couples who love each other and want to stay together with their offspring." Neither Will nor Nina was convinced by her adamant stance.

They both mumbled a hasty agreement with their friend that something would be sorted out. Then without warning Alice made *a comment that brought their platitudes to an abrupt halt, "Of course there's the tiniest possibility that I may not survive the childbirth. Don't look so shocked, both of you. It could happen. I'm being pragmatic."*

What on earth had made her come up with this notion? This certainly was not one of the factors that had entered the minds of either recipient of her news. She looked perfectly healthy. What was the deep rooted cause of this neurosis? Was she already ill and not prepared to tell them? Did she possess some sort of premonition? The answers to these questions came to light many months later, after the birth of her daughter.

"Now drink up. And then we'll have some lunch. You must tell me about how your lives are at the moment. We haven't had a chance for a chat for ages." And thus any questions regarding health issues were neatly quashed.

July 2305

Time moved forward: a continuum whose remorseless passage was measured by the constant click of each changing digit on the visual display unit above the corridor floor. Every hour, every minute, every second ticked like a pendulum demarcating the relentless beat of the building's daily routine. The clock-face of time controlled everyone's movement up and down the featureless corridor.

The only person that appeared not to be moving was Raymond Silva, a lone figure who sat slumped on one of the long cold grey benches that lined each wall of the Health and Well-being Centre's corridor. He had become accustomed to the whirring of the occasional intrusive, hovering drone pausing for inspection above his head and then flying off to scrutinise the presence of other civilians waiting for news of partners. Not that there were many other people in the Centre. The existence of loving family relationships had diminished drastically since the initiation of demarcated sectors within society, forcing people to lead far more isolated lives. Very few patients in the Centre could boast of having any visitors at all. But the love between Raymond Silva and his wife Alice was a thing of beauty and strength, only tested in recent months by Alice Silva's pregnancy.

Nursing staff in their drab grey uniforms padded up and down the corridor carrying various hand held monitors and scanners; small lights flashed on lanyards or from deep inside their breast pockets. The medical androids remained in the separate ward rooms. Androids were not as yet permitted to walk the corridors; there was still an undercurrent of concern regarding the potential power of these non-human beings in an establishment where there were vulnerable patients. The usefulness of automatons in all spheres of modern life was indisputable but their realms of influence needed to be monitored carefully. In the Health and Well-being centre, a clinical air of efficiency permeated the whole complex.

Then came a different sound: subtle but distinctive. It was the sound of the approaching physician's footsteps. Silva looked up and was beckoned into a nearby office to hear the news he had, up until that moment, patiently awaited yet dreaded. It was at this point that the patience exploded into a series of volcanic eruptions. The seemingly oblivious staff in the corridor continued with their work, but in the office the physician had to fend off the verbal blasts issuing from the eminent Mr Raymond Silva, Head of Government and Societal Communication.

The raised authoritarian voice, from a man who was accustomed to having his own way, reverberated around the usually calm office space, "My wife is the priority here. You must do everything within your power to keep her alive."

Although extremely nervous, the physician stood his ground, "With all due respect Mr Silva, we have an Official Governmental Form detailing that should there be any complications, the baby is to be saved. The form has been counter-signed by two of Alice Silva's trusted companions in the presence of The Governmental Tribunal, dated. . ."

"I do not care about any Official Governmental Form or any bloody Governmental Tribunal; we are talking about the life of a woman who is the wife of The Head of Government and Societal Communication. My wife. Surely my opinion has some influence here."

"I'm sorry sir, but. . ."

Silva reached forward, grabbed the paper from the physician, ripped it into shreds which he then threw into the air like

32

monochromatic confetti. He fully realised that electronic copies of all official forms were maintained in the records department, but his act of defiance offered him some degree of satisfaction, albeit rather a melodramatic gesture.

"That is what I think of your Official Form!"

The physician doggedly maintained his position, "Again I must urge you to comply with the wishes of your wife and to consider the life of your child. Your child's well-being is of paramount importance here. We can do nothing more for your wife. Even if she were to survive beyond this traumatic time her quality of life would be highly questionable."

Silva breathed heavily in a desperate attempt to calm his temper. "And who, may I ask, provided the birth assistance: incompetent humans or passionless androids?"

"I can assure you Mr Silva that all procedures carried out by humans are overseen by fully functioning and state of the art androids, and all procedures carried out by androids are overseen by humans whose expertise is unsurpassed. The risk of error is negligible."

Silva suddenly changed his approach, catching the physician in an unguarded moment. "Who signed the form?"

"A Mr William Alexander and his wife Nina Alexander, sir." *He immediately realised his mistake.*

Mr Raymond Silva turned and left.

The Legacy of Alice Silva

It transpired that all those months before, Alice had deliberately invited Will and Nina to a celebratory lunch knowing that her husband would be at work. She wanted them to sign an Official Government Form stating that should there be any complications at the time of birth, and it became a question of life or death for either the mother or the child, precedence should be given to saving the life of the child, not the mother. She had gone through all of the official channels. Ray knew nothing about this and although she had continued to insist that he was aware that they were having lunch with her, so she could give them the news, they were not to tell him about the form.

Will and Nina were embraced by a blanket of uncertainty. They truly believed that if Alice felt this strongly, surely she should discuss the situation with her husband; this is what each of them would have done. Somehow she persuaded them that it was unlikely to happen and she was probably just being neurotic and a decision of this kind would not actually be needed. Nina to this day could not fully remember how Alice had persuaded both of them, but she did and, almost inevitably, the unthinkable had happened. On that fateful day, when Alice Silva was ready to give birth, the life of a baby girl was spared; the life of the mother ended.

Raymond Silva never forgave either William or Nina Alexander.

Two days after Alice Silva's death, Raymond Silva arrived at the Alexanders' apartment. Only Nina was at home; this time it was Will who was out at work. When she opened the door, Silva stood there: an intimidating pillar of pure wrath. The dark eyes that she had once looked into with affection were now hardened stones of enmity. He thrust an envelope at her as if it were a fencer's epee. She instinctively stepped back in fear of her physical well-being.

"I have fulfilled my obligation to my wife to give you this. I owe you nothing more." He turned and started to stride away.

"Ray. Try to be reasonable. Will and I had no idea. . ."

He stopped and swung around in anger, "Don't ever dare to refer to me as Ray again. I am Mr Silva, The Head of Government and Societal Communication, and I would strongly advise you never to forget that."

As he walked down the road and out of sight, Nina stood and watched the man for whom she had previously held such strong affection. The envelope that had been thrust so viciously at her, remained in her hand and was now crumpled and twisted by her fists of anger and despair.

Nina took Alice's letter, written just a few days before her death, into her main living area. She sat down nervously. She carefully opened the envelope so as not to rip any of the contents and started to read. She read and reread the letter until the mass of words became an incomprehensible blur before her eyes, yet their meaning was devastatingly clear. Alice had recorded her thoughts and fears as the day of her daughter's birth approached.

It was heart wrenching.

My Dearest Nina and Will,

As I write this letter to you, I live in hope that you will never have the need to read my words. If, however, this is not the case and the letter has reached you, it means that I am no longer a part of your lives and my fears have been realised.

First of all I must genuinely apologise for exploiting, in the way that I did, the truly benevolent dispositions you both possess. Ray and I were desperate to have a child and I know that in the pressure of the moment, if a choice had to be made between my life and that of our greatest desire, Ray would make the wrong decision in the vain hope that our lives could carry on as normal. But that could never be; you must understand that our love has to be sealed and consummated with the birth of a longed for child.

You were not to know of my anxieties and fears; and you were not to know that, two years ago, I gave birth to a stillborn child: "an umbilical cord accident". Or at least that is what I was told. Remember Ray telling you that I had a virulent virus which necessitated isolation for a number of weeks?

At the time we thought it best to keep my pregnancy a secret from everyone. This would give us both the opportunity to come to terms with the enormity of our decision to have a family in the twenty-fourth century and how we would approach such an undertaking. Was there anyone better placed than the two of us to take on the bureaucracy that has violated our society so much in recent years?

As it turned out, no one actually needed to know. This time, however, I desperately wanted to tell someone and who better than my trusted friends of so many years? I'm afraid I underplayed the possibility of complications to you as I knew you would find it too difficult to sign that form. Please forgive me.

After the birth of our first child I was diagnosed as

35

having a stress disorder. This was caused by the trauma of having a stillborn baby, so I knew that I was taking a risk by becoming pregnant a second time. But the same thing couldn't happen again, surely? Ray and I were going to buck the system; we were going to be together as a complete family.

When I realised that I was pregnant once more, the feeling of joy was overshadowed by anxiety. I had lost one child; would I lose a second? Nightmares consumed my sleep. These nightmares became unbearable.

I did not want to put extra pressure on Ray so I told him that I was feeling a bit uncomfortable at night when trying to sleep. Because he had to work the next day, it was important for him to have a decent night's rest, so it was better for me to sleep in our spare room. I hid my intense anxiety from him; he didn't need that complication in his life.

As soon as I drifted off to sleep, the nightmares would begin. I would be lying on my back on a Health and Wellbeing Centre bunk. Grey clothed nursing staff and androids would be standing over me, speaking to me and pointing at me but I could not hear a word they said. Their voices were just muffled sounds reverberating around the room. I was convinced that I was going to die. They passed a red bundle to me to hold and I realised that the redness was blood. It was a dead baby wrapped in blood-stained blankets.

Invariably, I would wake up in the middle of the night in a panic, fully believing that I was in the Centre's ward. The bedclothes would, by this time, be lying in a heap on the floor and the sweat would be pouring from me. I was unable to move, convinced that intravenous drip feeds were attached to both of my hands and if I moved they would be torn from me.

I felt scared and alone. I didn't know who to talk to. In fact, I was too afraid to tell anyone - even you - fearing that I would be thought of as crazy.

Here I am and about to have a child. I want to live. I truly want to live. I am so scared but I know if anything should happen to me, a beautiful baby will have entered

this world and will be loved by Ray, and also by both of
you.

    I'll see you on the other side. Thank you for all you have
done.

    With love and affection,
        Alice

The tears flowed freely and unabated. Alice had never had the chance to hold that beautiful baby. Nina doubted that Raymond Silva would ever permit anyone else to hold that beautiful baby either, especially Nina and William Alexander. They were not even permitted to attend the funeral of their best friend.

Nina kept that letter for many years and her husband was the only other person who read it. She put it in the false base of a cabinet, hoping she would never have to read it or even look at it ever again. But the time did arrive when she felt the need to recover the letter and pass it on to someone whom she believed might be able to make some use of it, however insignificant.

2311: The Consequences

Six years later Nina herself became pregnant. She and Will were delighted and like Alice all those years before, they were prepared to spend as much time as possible together as a family of three. They never had the opportunity, but Silva's opportunity had arrived.

Unbeknown to them at the time, as soon as Raymond Silva discovered Nina's condition, she and her husband were condemned. Silva did all that he could to destroy them. There was nothing they could do; how could they fight against The Head of Government and Societal Communication? They never stood a chance.

William Alexander's defence lawyer was provided by the court and was merely a token of pseudo-authenticity; a Government puppet whose strings were controlled by men who kowtowed to Silva and his Governmental associates. Nina tried to explain to the lawyer how the circumstances that led to this situation had had a devastating effect on Mr Silva's emotional well-being which had been in a state of total imbalance since the death of his wife; that he blamed them for persuading the medical team to save the child and not the mother. She even showed him the letter and hoped that it could help their cause. The lawyer dismissed all her attempts with impunity.

Raymond Silva had not submitted a formal request to attend the criminal hearing and therefore it was a logical conclusion that he could not be that concerned. It was six years since his wife's death; no one holds a grudge for that length of time without doing anything about it beforehand. No one was that patient. And did she realise how dangerous it was to accuse such a high ranking Government official? He would deny being unaware of his wife's anxiety; how could he live with her and be oblivious to her stress? Alice's letter would not be of any value.

William Alexander was accused of theft and the handling and selling of illegal goods. He was also accused of threatening behaviour towards fellow citizens. The day of his trial arrived.

Nina sat silently in the benched area allocated for interested parties or people who had nothing better to do with their time than observe the sham, otherwise known as the legal process, afforded to the unfortunate plaintiff who in the twenty-fourth century was considered guilty until proven innocent. She despised the warped fascination people had for watching criminal sessions where there was an inevitability that the defendant would never leave by the front door ever again; an unjustifiable attraction for seeing others suffer. She had no idea who the other two people were that sat together three rows ahead of her, yet her suspicious eyes bore into the back of their heads with utter contempt.

The afternoon time slot for her husband's court session was three post meridiem; she had half an hour to anxiously await his trial.

She looked at every aspect of the austere room that surrounded her. An intrusive camera adorned each corner of the ceiling and at least five small air drones hovered at various strategic positions in the air above her head. One came so close to her that she was tempted to swat it away, but she could do nothing that might jeopardise the tiny, innocent being inside her.

The room had been a criminal court for as long as she could remember but at no time did she ever think that she would find herself caught in its venomous clutches. To the casual observer, the wooden panelling that enclosed the judiciary arena and separated it from the magistrate's elevated throne must have held an aesthetic beauty, but to Nina it confirmed an outmoded setting for an outmoded inquisition. The antiquated coat of arms on the wall behind where the presiding magistrate was to hold court had no relevance to the society in which she existed. Its incongruity was made all the more evident by the presence of two security androids standing to each side of it.

The presiding magistrate arrived in all his ceremonial paraphernalia. His superior gait clearly befitted the whole ritualistic situation.

Then William Alexander, who had been held in custody by Governmental authorities for four weeks prior to the hearing, entered the courtroom by a side entrance. He was escorted by two Governmental security firm representatives at precisely three o'clock. On seeing him, Nina gasped involuntarily at his appearance; he looked pale and haggard. She would not have recognised him if he had walked past her in the street; her own beloved husband was a shadow of his former self. She could not take her eyes off him.

The hearing was a mockery from beginning to end.

Each witness, on entering the stand, had a truth band attached to his wrist. In theory, this would inflict a searing electric shock to the wearer should his voice patterns and physical movement indicate that he was being untruthful. Although much was made of the attaching of the wrist band, it seemed strange to Nina that each witness was then permitted to let his arm hang down by his side, out of sight. Not once, during the whole proceedings did one man suffer from an electrical surge.

The first man to take the stand was huge, both in height and width. Her husband would have looked like a child in his presence, even before the debilitating four weeks he had spent in custody.

The presiding magistrate started to question the ogre. "Please state your name and relationship to the accused."

"I am Benedict Cooper. I worked with William Alexander as a service engineer for two years." Nina did not recognise him and had never heard his name mentioned by her husband who used to talk about his colleagues every evening when he got home.

"During that time did the accused ever offer you illicit goods?"

"Yes sir. He offered me ten flagons of alcohol at four brexemes per flagon. And said that he could provide the same amount again on a weekly basis."

"That is inexpensive for such sought after goods, I believe." Even the presiding magistrate seemed far from neutral in his approach.

"Yes sir. A flagon costs twelve brexemes in the Food Station. And, of course, no one is permitted to purchase more than one flagon per week."

"Did you take up this offer?"

"No sir." The mere suggestion was vehemently denied.

"Did you ask where he was getting the alcohol?"

"No sir. I didn't want to know."

"How did he react when you refused to take up his offer?"

"He told me I was a fool. It was good stuff and there was no way I could ever get into trouble for it. If anyone got into trouble, it would be him."

"He seems to have been right in that would you not say?"

"Yes sir."

"Did he ever threaten you?"

"Not me sir."

The thought of such a small man threatening such a huge bulk of a creature initiated a conspiratorial giggle from the two people sitting in front of Nina. It was soon stifled when the authoritarian gaze of the presiding magistrate pinpointed the source of the unwelcome interruption. At least he had made some attempt to carry out his allocated professional code of duty.

The evidence given by the second witness was much the same; as was that of the third, fourth and fifth witnesses. The only difference being that the fourth and fifth witnesses had apparently been threatened with violence. The fifth witness even showed a long angry red scar on his forearm extending from his elbow to his wrist which William Alexander had allegedly inflicted with the use of a kitchen knife.

Nina could not prove what was blatantly obvious to her, if not to anyone else: Raymond Silva had used his position of influence to coerce five separate men to testify against her husband. Whether his inducement was materially advantageous or threatening, Nina would never know or care. The pressure he put on them was frighteningly effective. It was bribery, pure and simple.

According to these five individuals, William Alexander sold illegal goods, such as drugs and illicit alcohol. He had no qualms whatsoever about the dire effect these substances could have on the vulnerable citizens of Lithport. He was also an aggressive man who would readily use violence as a means of persuasion.

Nina sat helplessly in court as these perfidious traitors described William Alexander as a thug, a bully, and a savage. After the fifth man gave his testimony, the treacherous character assassination was complete.

William Alexander was to be sent to the flatteringly named House of Detention for two years where he would learn the error of his ways and purge himself of all evil. He would then be fit and ready to undergo his execution by lethal injection. Occasionally, detainees were granted visits from family members or friends. This concession was denied William Alexander: his crimes were too heinous.

The eyes of the husband and wife met across the courtroom; he mouthed, "I love you" and was then escorted from the proceedings by two burly bodyguards and a small but intimidating House of Detention drone.

Nina Alexander sat in that court in stunned silence for two long hours after the case had finished. Then and only then, did she stand up and feel ready to face the world. The innocent life inside her would be loved and cherished like no other child before. Nina would not poison that child with anger and hatred. The child would be as perfect as any child could be.

As she left the court, a sneering voice came from the shadows behind her, "How does it feel to be alone?"

She turned with newly found power and confidence, "Raymond Silva, I will never be alone." She placed her hand on her rounded midriff, "And if you ever try to go anywhere near my child, you will have to get past me first. I will never stand by and watch you take my child from me."

He smiled, and for twelve years he went nowhere near her.

Reality

Chapter Three

A New Idea

For some reason Myra always believed that the apartment manager possessed an uncanny gift to deliberately visit her when she wanted to write. The residents in the block of apartments owned the greater percentage of their dwellings and it was up to them to look after their own properties, and yet the council seemed to feel that their twenty-five per cent ownership gave them the authority to send an apartment manager to inspect the buildings on a regular basis. It seemed a shame to Myra that they did not view other council commitments with such rigour. Or perhaps the apartment manager, a Mr Barrington-Smythe (or some other such similarly pompous double-barrelled name) just fancied her! And why not! He always seemed to be there at the most inconvenient of times and stayed with her longer than he stayed with any of the other residents.

Having finally managed to get rid of him, after the partaking of an alcoholic drink or two, she made herself a mug of coffee, went to the study and began to think about the next section of her manuscript.

Sitting at her computer desk, she briefly glanced out of the window. Below she saw the little girl wearing her customary old clothes: a khaki-green jumper that hung off her shoulders and sported a large hole in the elbow; a long pleated skirt that surely could not have been bought for her, passed down by an older sister perhaps; and dirty, scuffed leather ankle boots laced with string. A waiflike creature.

Today, the girl sat on the pavement playing with a rag doll. She rocked the doll to and fro in her arms as if comforting a baby. Then the doll, in her childlike mind, had clearly matured as she walked it in front of her holding each leg in her hands while the body flopped forward and backward.

As she played, a mother walked by pushing a buggy. The girl looked up and watched as the mother and child walked past; then, a few seconds later, something on the ground drew her attention away from the mother and her offspring. Lying askew in front of her was a brightly coloured cuddly bear in far better condition than her own plaything. She immediately realised that it had probably been dropped by the youngster in the buggy. Without a second thought, she jumped up and ran after the mother whilst holding the cuddly toy aloft and waving it in the air as if it was an aircraft marshalling wand. The briefly mislaid cuddly bear was duly returned to its owner and the girl's thoughtfulness was greeted with smiles and unerring gratitude.

Myra thought about her own childhood and had to be honest with herself that she would probably not have returned the infant's cuddly toy, but would have kept it for herself, telling her parents that she had found it on the ground somewhere. She would have had no misgivings about her economy with the truth; her tale would have been highly convincing and, without a hint of guilt, she would have gained a new toy.

The next day, Myra looked out again and watched the same girl. The rag doll had been abandoned and in its place was a game of hopscotch. This was quite surprising as Myra thought it to be a traditional game that had long since disappeared from streets and school playgrounds. There was the remembered symmetrical design chalked onto the pavement; she couldn't help but wonder where the chalk had come from. Each of the rectangles had a single cursive number in it ranging from one to eight. Myra tried to peer more closely to see what was used as the shooter. When she saw the morning sun glint on it she realised that it was a beer bottle top, probably abandoned the previous evening by a local teenage drinker, and then picked up by the young girl the next morning from a nearby gutter.

The girl threw the shooter into the first rectangle and nimbly hopped over it, landing with one foot in the second rectangle. She continued to hop to the end and back again, picking up the shooter on her return and jumping back to the beginning. The whole process was then repeated with the shooter being skilfully thrown into each square progressively up the numerical sequence.

When Myra was a little girl herself she would imagine that she was in an international competition where there was an adoring crowd who were chanting, "Myra. Myra. Myra." She would be about to break the world record at whatever activity she happened to be performing; it might be the number of times a football was bounced left-handedly without loss of control, or the number of times a tennis ball could be thrown against the wall and then caught, again without any loss of control. She contemplated as to whether this little girl also possessed a similarly ambitious imagination. So, when the boy on his skateboard came along; picked up the little girl's shooter; threw it across the road; and then skated off laughing, she wondered what the reaction would be and whether puerile anger would take over.

Myra recalled a time when she was a child skipping in the school playground with her friends watching her and counting the number of times she cleared the rope. It became a chant and she desperately wanted to reach one hundred skips: this, she decided, would be a new world record. "Ninety-four, ninety-five, ninety-six. . ." when suddenly that horrible boy, Billy Baines, had grabbed her skipping rope and run off with it shouting, "Sissy!" She pursued him relentlessly, weaving in and out of other children, going left, going right; she wouldn't give up. Eventually he stopped. He smiled at her with that mischievous glint in his eyes. He was puffing and panting, totally out of breath, and she walked calmly up to him and kicked him: hard. His whole body seemed to crumple and he burst into tears.

She turned her back on him and walked off; they were quits. Justice had been achieved: he had ruined her game and she had ruined his, or at least that is how she perceived the situation. It was not, as it transpired, to be the way it was perceived by others.

The following day, she discovered that Billy Baines' parents had phoned the school to complain about Myra's aggressive and unacceptable behaviour: she was clearly an uncontrollable child and this was not the first time she had bullied their poor son. Myra's protestations fell on deaf ears and she was given an after-school detention. She had to sit silently, on her own, and write out a hundred times, "I must behave like a young lady when playing". Actually this did not concern her as much as it might have done as she merely imagined that she was the world's best author. What really annoyed her was that she also had to write a letter of apology to that awful boy. As she sat there, fuming at the injustice of it all, she could see Billy walking out of the school gates, laughing and joking with his friends. She hoped her own parents would complain about him.

They didn't.

From that day forward she lost her faith in human nature. She hated all boys; they had always been bullies and always would be. And as far as adults were concerned, they seemed unprepared to listen, or even try to understand how she felt. What was the point of talking to people if they would not listen to her viewpoint?

She turned her attention again to the little girl on the street below. Having looked left and right, the girl then walked over into the road, picked up the beer bottle top, returned to the pavement and continued with her game of hopscotch. She was seemingly totally unconcerned by the interruption. She didn't chase after the skateboarder; she didn't seek vengeance for the way she had been treated. Two girls; two eras; two mindsets.

Myra's manuscript notes:

Introduction of new protagonist – young girl
    – clever, bright and unfazed – characteristics
    we can all aspire to
Clash of personalities
Apartment manager/Commissioner
Alcoholic bribery – male orientated

Fiction

The Manuscript
Part Three

2323: The Present

Tania

Tania Alexander, a young girl not yet twelve years old, sat on the wide windowsill, her arms embracing her lower legs, her chin resting on her knees. She pulled the curtain back far enough to see that he was there again.

It was time. She glanced briefly towards her bedroom clock and turned her head again to look out of the window. Her whole being was alert; brought into focus by an overriding sense of calm, silent expectation.

The lamp at the street corner shed a cone of light onto the man, trilby hat just pulled down far enough to mask his face, black gabardine mackintosh following the contours of his body down to his calves. He pushed his right hand into his pocket, took out a packet of 'Ye Olde Cigarettes' from which he selected one before replacing the packet into his pocket, having put the chosen cigarette into his mouth. Smoking e-cigarettes was not for him; he felt they lacked panache. He was actually surprised that they were a permissible indulgence in this puritanical world of which he was a part. He waited a few seconds, as always, and then with a couple of flicks of the lighter, he tilted his head back and the cigarette smoke curled up towards the lamplight. Tania could sense his relaxation; she could feel his nerves calming. But at no time was she ever able to get a really good look at his face. She had no idea who he was, but she knew he possessed an aura of calmness and self-control.

He looked forward again, continued smoking for the regulatory sixty seconds, threw what was left of his cigarette down, rolled the ball of his right foot over it, looked to the left, looked to the right, put both hands into his pockets, walked down Berkeley Street and was gone. The whole procedure had lasted no more than four minutes. It never did.

"Are you getting ready for bed now, darling?" Tania's mother called from downstairs. She did not need to call, but she wanted to confirm the innate sense of closeness between mother and daughter. She gradually ascended the steps and reached the top just as her beautiful daughter replied.

"Yes, Mum."

"Looking out of the window again? Anything exciting?"

"No."

Her mother smiled with that inexplicable omniscient demeanour she had always possessed. "Good night darling." She leaned over, gave Tania a kiss on the forehead and left her to take herself to bed.

Tania drew the curtains back across the window and jumped off the sill, landing softly on the floor. She had never been a noisy child; she could walk up behind people and they would not realise that she was there until she actually spoke. But she rarely did that either. She was a quiet girl who didn't need to ask people how they felt; she just knew. She was tired now. It would be another dull twenty-four hours until she saw him again. Daily life held no challenge for her and she needed to be challenged. One day she would call out to him, or even go out to speak to him. There was some goodness there; she could feel it deep in his inner core. He wasn't a bad man, but he was an enigma. He held a secret within him: a secret which permeated his whole demeanour. And what was he doing frequenting the Female Sector so openly every evening?

"Mum?"

Her mother had not gone far. In fact she had only taken one step outside of the room and paused just beyond the doorway at the top of the staircase. She immediately returned. "Yes?"

"You know the man don't you?"

"Yes I do." Her mother was not at all surprised by the unprompted question and had no need to ask Tania to specify what man she was trying to identify.

"Who is he?"

"His name is Mr Raymond Silva and he is the Head of Government and Societal Communication." She paused and then added with some sense of regret, "And he was once a very good friend."

Tania could sense the heavy shadow of sadness that overwhelmed her mother's thoughts; she did not wish to encroach upon her mother's feelings and further upset her.

No more questions were asked but the young girl was totally aware of the significance of the word "once" in her mother's response.

Kilman

The crime figures for June 2323 showed yet another dramatic and highly gratifying decrease. Kilman looked at the computer screen and smiled; his elite force of Special Service Patrols was doing a good job. They monitored and protected every sector with total confidence.

In the Male Sector, the explicit use of weaponry had proven to be highly effective and any menial workers who held ambitions of being big shots in the criminal underworld were soon cut down to size. Kilman was ruthless.

In the Female Sector, rogue male street-walkers had almost completely disappeared. Kilman, however, was a little curious about one aspect for which he could not provide a completely satisfactory explanation: emergency contact always came far more promptly than he would have thought possible, almost before anything had even occurred. It was as if the women knew that there was a potential threat. And the emergency contact always came from the women in the sector, never from his patrolling servicemen asking for backup. How did the women know there was a stranger in their vicinity? Did they have a neighbourhood watch scheme of which he was unaware? Admittedly the walls of their apartments were thin; any loud sound from the adjoining property could be easily heard. And all the apartments had windows looking out onto the street so strangers would soon be detected. He shrugged his shoulders. If the crime figures were going down, why worry? He did, however, fleetingly consider the effectiveness of the present procedures for the Elevation Test.

In the Couple Sector, where he himself lived, there were clearly no issues. Crime figures had never been high in this sector; the threat of immediate confinement or banishment was enough to quell any of the petty arguments that tended to occur between the women while their partners were at work. The women stayed at home and kept their households clean, tidy and well organised. Some of them employed the help of domesticated androids, but very few did this; there was still an innate distrust of these machines and with all the time women had on their hands, there was no need to employ them. Nothing was out of place in this sector.

Obviously, when the men were out at work, the women would contact each other during the day on their landline telephones, but Kilman knew that their conversations purely focused on what he dismissively termed 'women talk': physical appearance and beautification. Women were so superficial. There were certainly no sinister issues there; Visual Display Screens were present in all of the apartments for when the Government needed to communicate with the general public, but censorship of computer communication had reached a point where the ruling Official Government possessed total control and could access all channels with ease. He looked forward to a time when all of the screens had the capacity for two-way visualisation, but perhaps this was a step too far, possibly even providing the opportunity to participate in observation of a carnal nature. He had to admit that it had been cyber bullying building up for years that had brought about the restrictions in the use of social electronic media.

There was no other media activity. Women's rights movements had become so rife during the twenty-first century that men had had to take a stand against the feminine flow, even if the measures employed were, at times, quite brutal.

Mr Raymond Silva, Kilman's immediate superior and Head of Government and Societal Communication, would be pleased to see this new set of figures. The data spoke for itself: the whole city was in a state of balance. In fact, his superior had just arrived at his office door following his unexplained daily visit to the Female Sector. One day Kilman would ask about that, but for the moment he concerned himself with other matters and dutifully called across the corridor and beckoned him in.

Silva removed his coat, opened his office door, threw the black gabardine coat onto the back of a chair and reluctantly returned to his deputy's office. He entered the room and stood behind Kilman, looking over his shoulder at the visual display unit before them.

Smugly, Kilman leant back on his chair; he detected the whiff of cigarette smoke of which he disapproved but said nothing. Twirling a pen between his fingers, he spoke with an assumed arrogance that went hand in hand with his unshakable conviction, "We deserve a pat on the back, don't you think?"

Silva had never really liked his deputy that much but he certainly could not fault the man's dedication to his job. As he stood there staring at the screen, he longed for another cigarette or a large glass of whisky. Kilman's next words brought him abruptly out of his reverie.

"This sector is now fully under control. I believe we can extend into the outer regions, beyond The Wall. We cannot just sit here ignoring the possibility of attack." He looked surreptitiously towards his senior for signs of any response. "I've heard there are rebellious autochthonous elements in the outer regions. They could attack at any time: over The Wall, through The Wall, or even under The bloody Wall." Silva was always irritated by Kilman's use of elaborate language, intended to impress yet mixed with deliberately crude abruptness; it seemed to belie his uncompromising and unequivocal character.

Although clearly ambitious, Silva's deputy had never struck him as being either imaginative or driven by anything other than wanting to metaphorically step into Silva's shoes when he finally made the decision to take his well earned early retirement. He truly believed that his deputy would just bide his time. He really didn't think he would deliberately set himself a target that was not attainable in the short term.

He slowly placed his hands in his pockets, grunted quietly, turned away and, without any real commitment, mumbled "Possibly" under his breath. He needed to get back to the sanctuary of his office; Kilman's office was cold and clinical. Most of the offices held at least one photograph of a loved one from the Couple Sector, either in a digital frame on a desk or hanging from the wall. Photographs of any offspring that might belong to any single members of staff had been banished. When children left a domicile at the age of twelve, they left for ever and were to be forgotten. Some of the offices sported a work of art that had been ratified by the ruling party. Kilman's had nothing.

Just as Silva reached the door, that officious, grating voice broke the silence again. "I hope you don't mind but I've made some further calculations and we can easily afford to send an elite squad out for reconnaissance. They will be fully armed, of course. A series of short forays over the next few weeks should be enough to assess the situation."

"Starting when?"

"Friday."

Three days' time. This man really was prepared. Silva did not need this. "Send your plans by nine o'clock in the morning. I will look at them during the day tomorrow. Do not take any action without my knowledge or permission. You must wait until I get back to you."

Kilman was satisfied. He had rattled the cage.

Raymond Silva

Silva returned to his office. His temper had been awoken. "Damn that man!" His dark eyes burned with anger; he clenched his fists and hunched his shoulders forward as if he was a pugilist about to start a fight in the boxing ring. He thumped his hand onto his desk and then walked hurriedly to his office cupboard. He couldn't smoke here as the detectors would immediately pick up the fumes. Perhaps he couldn't even risk a drink. No one, not even the Head of Government and Societal Communication, knew where every hidden camera was lurking. But why should he worry? Everyone knew that he kept whisky in his office. What would happen anyway? He would receive a pathetic warning and then life would carry on as per normal.

He took a small shot from the whisky decanter put aside for 'special guests': those whom he needed to impress. There were governors from other walled communities and, most significant of all, the omnipotent Commissioner for the south west townships of the country who as it so happened would be visiting the next day to inspect Lithport's facilities. Gradually his taut nerves began to relax and he sat down, thinking about his next steps. Calmness was his forte; anger did not suit his public persona.

Kilman needed to be diverted. Forays to the south of the township would not do any harm, but how could he ensure that Kilman's men went in this direction? No, he had to do something else. For a moment, a sense of complete helplessness descended upon him.

He could not really do anything the next day because the Commissioner's visit was the focus of attention, but perhaps arrangements could be made for something the day after that. Yes, Thursday would be ideal. Of course, it had to be an apartment raid on a possible Elevationist; that would certainly suffice. But whose apartment?

It didn't take him long to make the decision. The raid would be a little sooner than he had anticipated; he was not entirely convinced that his suspicions were fully justified, but better sooner than not at all and risk Kilman getting in his way. He really didn't like that man. There was no finesse in anything he did, whereas Silva thought of himself as having at least a degree of discernment in his dealings with civilians.

The Commissioner's Visit

Two shots of whisky for each of them and Silva was ready to show the Commissioner upstairs to the final 'pièce de résistance' as he liked to call the rooftop attack force machinery. Or, at the very least, he was ready; he was not so sure about the Commissioner. He looked down at the two glasses: his was empty; the Commissioner's was still full. Hopefully the hospitality bit had not been overdone. The Commissioner certainly didn't look as though he was in any hurry to drink the second glass.

For some unknown reason, in his mind's eye, Silva briefly visualised the Commissioner drunkenly inspecting the beautiful machinery above, lurching towards the control panel and flying one of the machines; soaring over the rooftops, sweeping outside of the walled township, diving downwards and spooking any creature below. But then again, he could not really imagine this man ever losing enough self control to become drunk. Even his name conjured up a man from a bygone era who would only ever drink his high quality whisky from a tiny pure crystal glass, whilst standing in front of an old open wood fire, one arm casually resting on a mantelpiece, the other holding a long pipe that was merely a prop but never smoked. Sir Charles Bartholomew-Spence, what sort of ridiculous name was that?

His musings were interrupted, "Are we ready, Silva?" A question stated with a clear, slightly mocking, emphasis on his subordinate's name.

"Yes, of course. I do apologise. Perhaps you would like to take your whisky with you."

The look of disdain told its own story, "No, I think that I will leave it here. One glass is amply sufficient." Said, of course, with a poignant look at Silva's second empty glass.

In reality, Charles Bartholomew-Spence was far more understanding and approachable than Silva had ever given him credit for. He actually viewed Silva with mild amusement, knowing that his visits would always be accompanied by a glass or two, or even, on occasions, three of whisky. They would be consumed by Silva, but not by Mr Bartholomew-Spence; not that he viewed his subordinate as an alcoholic, in fact he had a lot of respect for Silva, who had always been a highly effective Head of Government. The man had been devastated by the death of his wife, but had seemed to rally in recent years. Charles Bartholomew-Spence even hoped that there was the calming influence of another woman on the horizon, but he did not feel that such a conversation was appropriate to their working relationship.

Like his character, the Commissioner's clothes were a uniform to be worn with a sense of duty as to the occasion. His smart appearance reflected that duty; all who knew him expected a smart appearance. No one ever thought about where he went when that duty was over. He returned to his own world; no one ever expected to see him in theirs. He arrived, seemed to command the very air that surrounded him and left. Time had chiselled his face and every line might have a story to tell, but no one asked. He walked with a discernible limp from previous military action, but no one knew exactly what had happened, and no one asked.

The two men had spent the morning in the laboratories and the various offices; Silva had answered with skill and competence any queries that the Commissioner elicited from him. They had had lunch and now they had had their whisky of the finest quality. Silva closed his eyes for a moment and let the inner warmth course through his body. He felt energised: whether this was the effect of the beautiful golden liquid or the prospect of seeing those machines once again, he was not sure, but the day seemed to be going well. He had also managed to give Kilman so much work in preparation for the next day, that he was out of the way and unable to interfere.

Silva and Charles Bartholomew-Spence entered the lift. The doors whispered to a close behind them and they were soon ascending to the zenith of the building. Nothing was said, and within a short space of time they reached their destination and the doors whispered again to reveal a huge room full of artillery capable of attacking an enemy at a moment's notice. The roof would slide back to expose the open sky; the machines could rise into the air and speedily fly to their allotted destination. A selected few individuals had the authority to control these machines: the overall authority rested on the shoulders of the Commissioner. Others included Silva, Kilman with Silva's permission, and one other of whom both Silva and Kilman were totally unaware. Charles Bartholomew-Spence was no fool.

The Commissioner immediately recognised the almost manic passion Silva seemed to have for these machines. Oh, he hid his passion very well, but it was there.

"We have, of course, maintained these machines with great care, Commissioner. Every one of them is primed and ready to be put into active operation at a moment's notice. I take pride in this elite force."

It seemed strange to the Commissioner that a group of machines should be referred to as an 'elite force', a phrase that he would personally prefer to attach to a group of men not a group of machines.

Silva caressed the shiny surface of the nearest military air-drone, "No one dare attack us." His voice reflected the pride that was clearly evident in every cell of his body.

Charles Bartholomew-Spence now looked at Silva with

interest in order to discern any reaction to his next comment, which would probably be received with little if any enthusiasm.

"We live in an age of peace and mutual respect as you know Silva. I doubt very much whether any of these machines will ever again be flown in anger and I am considering decommissioning at least ninety per cent of them if not all of them. They seem to me to be an unnecessary expenditure."

Silva visibly staggered a step or two backwards but soon gained his self-control. "Oh, I see. Has this been a committee decision, sir?"

"It has." There was a clear sense of finality in the tone of his voice.

Even Silva fully realised that at this point he was unwise to question the decision.

"You do not approve. You have, after all, cherished these machines for many years."

Silva swallowed, "I have. But my duty is to serve."

So was that the end of it all? Charles Bartholomew-Spence was pragmatic enough to believe that would probably not be the case; Silva was pragmatic enough to actually know that would not be the case.

Reality

Chapter Four

Alone

Myra could not understand why she was dreaming so much in bed at night; this worrying situation had been going on for months. She had never dreamt so excessively in her life before, having never had any trouble switching herself off from the concerns of the day, and subsequently falling into a night of deep recuperative slow wave sleep. But now it meant that every morning she was waking up absolutely exhausted. Surely sleeping should help recharge the batteries: a deep and physically resting revitalisation process, not a night full of amorphous dreams absorbing all her energy.

She was becoming very anxious. The extreme stress overload seemed to be undermining her ability to distinguish between dreaming reality and the real world, yet she would still not admit to anyone, least of all herself, that she needed specialist help. Her dreams, although seemingly chaotic, always appeared to focus on her inadequacies as a mother. On this particular night she had been lying on the floor of the church in a drunken stupor. Miriam, smoking a cigarette, was strapped into a flying buggy, circling above her. Then another Miriam appeared above her in a flying buggy; this time the small baby was burbling incomprehensibly on a mobile phone. Then a third Miriam appeared, holding a toy aeroplane and shooting randomly at all the icons in the church. While the three Miriams flew above her head, the young church verger stood imperiously above her. His hands were placed firmly on his hips. Scowling, he looked down at her in disgust, "You should be ashamed of yourself. Call yourself a mother. Your children are out of control."

She awoke, totally drained.

It had been two weeks since Myra had seen the little girl playing across the road opposite her apartment and she just could not understand what had happened to her. Where had she gone?

Myra sat at her inactive but quietly purring computer. Her notebook and pen lay idle to one side with a few spidery scribbles adorning the pages. She looked up at the pin-board in front of her but her mind was blank; nothing was coming to her. How on earth could she stumble at this early hurdle?

Then she heard a welcome sound; the bang, bang, bang of ball against wall. She could not have been happier, but when she moved the curtain slightly to one side to see her young friend, it was not a girl she saw but a boy. It was the boy that she had seen throw the hopscotch shooter across the road.

She decided to go and talk to him. Perhaps he knew where the little girl had gone. Miriam was asleep and even if she woke up, she could not go anywhere. The baby was not yet able to get out of her cot, and Myra hoped that this situation would last for some time to come.

It took only a minute to make her way outside; finding herself unusually free from the hindrance of her daughter's buggy, she did not even need to use the lift.

"Hi there. Wow, you're a skilful footballer." A compliment was probably a good way to begin.

The boy, who must have been about ten to eleven years old, eyed her suspiciously, "S'pose you want me to go and kick the ball somewhere else."

"No, not at all. I was looking out of my window up there and admiring your skills. Do you play with a local boys' football club?"

The boy still eyed her suspiciously and did not bother to answer; it was as if he realised that there was an ulterior motive to her sudden appearance. She decided to just broach the true reason for going down to speak with him. "There's usually a little girl playing here. I don't suppose you know where she's gone? It's just that the other day when she ran an errand for me I made a promise that I would buy her some sweets, but I forgot the type of sweets she liked so I was going to ask her before buying them. She might have some sort of allergy that I don't know about." Lying had always come easily to Myra.

The word 'sweets' seemed to have a significant effect on the young lad. "Oh that'd be Tina. She's gone. And won't be back." The boy clearly sensed an opportunity. "I could run an errand for you."

"I'll bear that in mind. This particular small errand, though, has already been done but I never got the chance to give her any sweets."

He cleverly tried another approach; Myra could not fault his tenacity. "I could give 'em to 'er."

"Really! Even though you have just told me that she won't be coming back. And you being the boy who I happened to see throw her hopscotch shooter across the road."

This caught him off guard. "It were only a bit o' fun. A laugh."

"Tell me where she's gone and I'll remember your offer when I need some help in the future."

"She got took away. Her mam topped 'erself. Overdosed. Couldn't cope, my mam said. So 'er kid was taken by the council or welfare, or somethin' like that. Once they found her. My mam said they searched the house high and low and eventually found 'er hiding in the cupboard under the stairs. That would've been the first place I would've looked. I've seen Harry Potter. Won't see 'er again now. Mind you, she might get adopted by some rich family and that'd be good for 'er, wouldn't it?"

"And there's no father?"

"Oh, Big Billy, he's in the nick for GBH. He always claimed he was framed but he's done it before so he got four years I think. He even said it was a mate who grassed on him." The matter of fact way in which all of this was said slightly unnerved Myra and she could not help but wonder if this Big Billy was the Billy whom she had known at school. She fleetingly hoped it was: retribution at last. There were, however, other more pressing thoughts in her head.

She was unsure how to reply to the young lad so, mumbling her gratitude, she turned and walked back towards her flat.

He called after her. "What about them sweets? I told you what you wanted to know."

"Another time."

A vertical middle finger aimed at her back was accompanied by, "Silly cow!" shouted out after her with all the contempt he could muster. He even considered kicking his football at her head just for target practice, but he thought that he might not get it back from her and it was a new ball, given to him my his mother for running some errands.

When she returned to her apartment, Myra actually began to feel more upbeat about the girl's disappearance. Yes she could use this. She was not really interested in Big Billy's incarceration; she had already included a court scene in her manuscript. Not lost on her, however, was the irony of there being a sense of collusion and deceit in both the real and the fictional worlds. This was clearly meant to be: a poetic parallel. She went back to her computer, made a few manuscript notes and then started typing enthusiastically, totally oblivious to the plaintive cries from the next room. Baby Miriam had probably been woken up by the voices raised in anger permeating through from the adjacent apartment. The Mortnels were arguing again.

Myra's manuscript notes:

Mother's love
Girl disappears
Where does she go?
Cupboard under stairs?
Where next?
Someone takes her
Keep undercurrent of male domination/brutality
The Kilmans

Fiction

The Manuscript
Part Four

The Final Days of Childhood

There was a moist and welcoming breeze in the air today; the authorities had clearly decided that the past few days had been stifling hot and the citizens deserved some alleviation from the oppressive atmosphere. It was one of Tania's daily journeys to the Institute. As she made her way along her chosen route, she recalled times when she was a tiny child; she had never possessed a big stature and even now, she was the smallest in her class. When younger, she had always made every journey fun. She would skip along, walk, run, crouch down and creep forward looking from side to side for make-believe enemies. She imagined that secret agents were shadowing her and she set herself targets to get to her destination before being captured. The Institute was her safe haven.

She would hide in the LED lampposts' slivers of shadow, formed from the quasi-sun above, and run between each one, trying to get there before any Government vehicle overtook her. She would lean up against the walls of buildings and sidle sideways until she reached a junction that needed to be crossed. She would try to somehow hide inside her Government Issue uniform to make herself look inconspicuous. It had all been such fun. But not anymore.

She still did many of these things; but they had become a necessary habit. There was no longer any fun involved. Today, as always, she looked for the Government vehicles, the cameras perched high up on the rooftops and the occasional drone flying, often hovering furtively overhead. Instinctively she stayed close to the walls, always in the shadows, always alert; but it wasn't a game anymore. It was reality. Her mother had told her that Government officials, specifically employed to spy on the citizens, camped out in buildings; every citizen of Lithport was monitored closely. It was inevitable that one day androids with their beady, lifeless yet ever alert eyes would be permitted to patrol the streets.

Tania never took the same route two days in a row; her journey rarely followed the same pattern. Although she always ensured that she was never late for the Institute – the consequences of that would be dire – she also ensured that she did not arrive at exactly the same time: a minute here, a few minutes there, anything up to half an hour early felt safe, more than that might seem suspicious.

On this particular day, she had noted four extra government vehicles sliding quietly and stealthily past. Two extra drones hovered in the skies above and it seemed unusually difficult to avoid the ever searching cameras which, she was sure, appeared to hone almost imperceptibly yet noticeably in her direction.

On occasions like these there were often fewer students in class the next day; empty spaces that had not been there before seemed to cry out and Tania wondered where those girls had gone and whether she would ever see them again. Little did she realise that her own spot would prove to be the next empty space for others to wonder about, if indeed they did any significant thought processing. The absences had become such a regular occurrence that Tania's classmates had stopped reacting, perhaps just like herself their mothers had told them not to react but to stay as inconspicuous as possible. The girls around her seemed to have become so mechanical, as if their very souls had been sucked out of them, that she began to wonder whether she was the only one who ever really noticed the changing numbers.

Not only would her space be empty the next day, but it would be empty for a long, long time. In fact: forever.

Boys did not attend this particular Institute; they were 'educated' elsewhere, or more accurately, they were indoctrinated elsewhere. Tania was not fully aware of what

61

happened in the boys' establishment but she often inwardly questioned the learning at the girls' Institute; however, her mother told her never to question the instructor. She was never to make her presence truly felt, but was to blend into the room just as she blended into the walls and lampposts on the journey there.

The girls' education mainly comprised: knowing how to be a law abiding citizen; understanding the societal roles of a female in Lithport; and etiquette. The topics that formed Tania's education were doctrinal. Nothing creative was permitted and fictional literature had been banned many years previously. Learning to read was part of the system, but learning to read only the official literature that was permitted and authorised by the Government; nothing else. Tania yearned for the wonderful stories her mother told her or even read to her when she was able to acquire an illicit text. Tania eagerly consumed the writings of Terry Pratchett, Garth Nix, Michelle Magorian, Philip Pullman and Joanne Kathleen Rowling, to name but a few of her favourites.

Each instructional day started and ended with spoken allegiance to the Government and, other than in class, no groups of three or more students were allowed to stand together anywhere within the confines of the Institute. Students left the building at the end of the day individually at thirty second intervals; the drones and cameras ensured that they did not meet up beyond that. All students in class were addressed by a number followed by the initial letter of their actual name; this was the one concession to personal identity made by those in authority. Personal names were for use at home and for adults only. Tania's label in the Institute was 48T.

Today the instructor demanded that the leaving procedure would be in alphabetical order of each individual's final letter label. The procedure changed on a daily basis so that no one could predict the order in which the girls would leave the premises. The instructor was an austere looking woman who wore the same uniform every day and whose authority in the class was absolute. Tania detected a touch of humility, but it was certainly a characteristic that the instructor did not manifest deliberately or openly.

Today, as always, all the girls stood patiently in the chosen obligatory sequence: 102A, 35C, 64D, 69D and so on, with Tania at the end of the queue to depart, being the only girl whose name began with the letter T. The instructor paced with uncharacteristic nervousness up and down the silent line; no talking was ever permitted at this time. Tania had sensed her instructor's nerves becoming increasingly fraught as the day progressed, but she did not know why. Finally, Tania was the last girl in the yard and it was her turn to leave; a surreptitious hand gently slipped a small scrap of paper into the young girl's pocket, accompanied by an urgently whispered comment, "For your mother, Tania." Tania was shocked to hear herself referred to by her true name but successfully managed not to show it. In fact, unbeknown to her, she would never be referred to as 48T ever again. She briefly looked up at her instructor who faced forward as if nothing out of the ordinary had occurred. Tania left.

The instructor whispered quietly to herself, "Good luck little one." She turned and re-entered the institute without further comment; she had done her duty.

Tania was a sensible but curious child, and there was no way that she would refrain from having a furtive look at the note as soon as the opportunity arose.

She walked off at a reasonable pace until she found a deep shadow in which to hide. She looked up and down the roadway; she looked skyward and then above into the windows of nearby buildings. Finally satisfied, she removed the note from her pocket.

'Tst brght frwrd tnght t 8.00. b wrnd.'

The 'code', such as it was, could easily be deciphered and would not have fooled anyone. Tania knew that tonight was two weeks early and she deeply regretted that, but there was nothing that she could do about it. She would be taken away for her Elevation Test. The time had arrived. There would be no escape.

She got home slightly later than usual, and when she entered the apartment, she passed the note over to her mother who immediately read it nervously, her hands shaking involuntarily. The fear was palpable; the dramatic all-embracing hug was instantaneous. They both knew what was to come; they had talked about it and had decided that when the time came and if no other arrangements had been made, their evening routine was to remain the same. And so it did.

Confirmation of Dreaded Anticipation

Tania had gone upstairs at about seven o'clock that evening, leaving her mother to her own thoughts. Nina Alexander's mind was a mixture of deep affection for her daughter, for her late husband and for her many friends, among whom she would once have counted both Raymond Silva and his wife Alice. It was with a profound sadness that she could no longer consider that to be the case: Alice had died in childbirth eighteen years previously and her husband had since become a man whom she just did not recognise as the person he once was. Those heart wrenching past experiences had served to influence her resolve.

The Challenge Begins

It was time. The artificial light was gradually fading. The authorities should have organised rain today, not sunlight; the idea of pathetic fallacy was clearly alien to them. Tania glanced briefly towards her bedroom clock and turned her head again to look out of the window. She wondered, on this special evening, whether he would actually be there or whether she would never see him again.

The lamp at the street corner shed a cone of light onto the man, trilby hat just pulled down far enough to mask his face, black gabardine mackintosh following the contours of his body down to his calves. He started rubbing his hands together and blowing on them; he moved from one foot to the other to counteract the cold, or that is what people who did not know his routine would have thought if they had just been walking by, but this man never felt the cold. Tania realised that he wasn't cold. He knew tonight was different; he was nervous. She could feel it. She straightened her back, eyes fixed intently upon his next move.

He pushed his right hand into his pocket, took out a packet of cigarettes from which he chose one before replacing the packet into his pocket, having put the chosen cigarette into his mouth.

Tania started to feel a little more at ease again. He waited a few seconds, as always, and then with a couple of flicks of the lighter the cigarette smoke curled up towards the lamplight. But he did not tilt his head back and she could not feel his relaxation. Tania did not feel frustrated today; she felt fearful. She knew it was the same man, but something was different; and she felt somehow betrayed that he was involved with her approaching Elevation Test. Then he suddenly turned and ran. He ran towards her home!

There was a thunderous crashing of the front door, men shouting and the smashing of crockery downstairs. She had been so busy concentrating on the man in the lamplight that she had not detected the others arriving at her home. She was angry with herself for being so foolish, but now she had to react and react quickly. She knew the drill; she had practised it so many times before.

Her thought processes jettisoned into action. She reached out for her mother, but suddenly and inexplicably realised that she could no longer feel her comforting presence, yet she knew that she had been downstairs. Her mother was gone. Without a sound, Tania instinctively jumped from her windowsill like a tiger pouncing noiselessly towards its prey. She knew exactly what she had to do.

There was a lot of scuffling and men's voices. A sense of urgency filled the house and an overly dominant stage whisper hushed everyone, demanding quiet, until eventually an expectant silence embraced the whole house. Within that silence was an almost imperceptible sound: Tania recognised the familiar creak of the third stair leading up to her bedroom.

The door to Tania's room slowly opened. Silva walked in, his small stun pistol remained secreted in his pocket, hidden from public view. He didn't want to frighten the girl further; she must already be feeling intensely nervous. He quietly spoke her name as he entered the room, "Tania?"

There was no reply.

For the moment, he was not unduly worried. Why should she answer a stranger's voice? She was probably curled up on her bed in the corner of her room, absolutely petrified. But she wasn't. She wasn't in the room at all.

His voice rose, "Tania?"

He looked around the room and its overwhelming pinkness.

Despite the seriousness of the situation, he could not help but smile at this: light pink walls, dark pink curtains and a matching dark pink bed cover. The bedside cabinet had a digital framed picture of the girl's mother embracing her daughter, both smiling at the camera. For some reason he wondered briefly who had taken the photograph. By the side of the photograph frame was a small box; he opened it to be greeted by tinkling music as a plastic ballerina rose out of the box to pirouette around and around until she gradually slowed and finally came to a halt; the internal mechanism groaned and whirred into silence. The chipped paint on the ballerina's face made her look almost manic, an evil clown laughing at his vain attempt to find the girl. He slammed down the lid of the box. It was a relic of a bygone era: a touch of sentimentality. Just like all the gaudy, unnecessary pinkness surrounding him.

Where was she? He leant down and quietly spoke her name again as he pulled back the sheets and looked beneath the bed. He pulled out the boxes from underneath, but there was nothing, only the accumulated dust of weeks without thorough cleaning and a handful of forgotten ribbons and hairgrips. But no Tania.

He turned and saw the wardrobe; this was the only place left in the bedroom for her to be hiding. He pulled back the doors; he was beginning to become very irritated now. He tugged at the clothes that hung inside and threw them across the room. Her name, scribbled across the back of the wardrobe in a black felt tip marker pen, mocked him. In anger, he pulled at the doors and had to jump quickly out of the way as the whole lot fell crashing to the floor. Where was she? There was nowhere left to hide and yet she was not there.

He looked up to see if there was an attic entrance. Of course, there wasn't: Female Sector houses and apartments were deliberately designed without outdated lofts or attics. Attics had only been used years ago for Christmas decorations and holiday suitcases; people no longer celebrated the outmoded Christmas festival or went on holiday. There was no reason for any building to have an attic. It would have been far too tempting an invitation for illicit communication.

He stood, frustrated, in the middle of the room, surrounded by the mess that he himself had created. She must have gone out through the bedroom window. He walked across the room and

66

tried to pull up the sash; it was locked from the inside. He unlocked it and pulled up the heavy frame. It was too heavy for a young girl, and how could she have escaped and locked it from the inside? He called down to his men, more in hope than certainty, "Did she climb out of the window? Can you see her? Have you got her?"

"No," came the voice from below, answering all three questions with the one monosyllabic response that he did not want to hear.

"Are you sure?" Of course he knew that they were sure and his question was ridiculous. He turned back to the room without even waiting for the reply. He strode purposely over to the bedroom door and called down to Kilman, "She's not here!"

Kilman stood at the bottom of the stairs. Lying at his feet was Tania's dead mother. There was no blood. No sign of any struggle. But she was undoubtedly dead. She had fulfilled her promise to Silva: she had not stood by and watched him take her child from her.

"She must be." Kilman stormed angrily up the stairs, crashing into the corner wall where the stairway turned. Four more steps and he was facing Silva. "Where the bloody hell is she?"

No elaborate language this time Silva noted, and this seemed to have a calming effect on him. "If I knew the answer to that question, I would have found her." His eyes were level with those of Kilman; it was the latter who turned away first, but Silva continued as the man in front of him walked back down. Silva knew that his deputy wanted to check the room, to check that some obvious hiding place had not been overlooked. "We'll put an around the clock watch on the place. She'll turn up. Perhaps she has been staying with a friend." But he knew this was not the case; he had seen her in her usual spot up on the windowsill.

"And it looks as though her mother won't be able to tell us." Any subtle sense of irony was lost on his deputy, so he turned to the men searching for whatever they could find, not really knowing what they were looking for; they had never had to search for a missing child before. "Clear up this place and we will continue close surveillance from outside, even if it takes all week. I am sure you can organise that, Kilman." Again, any subtlety in his tone of voice was lost on his deputy.

Kilman carried out a final sweep of the house. Silva left. He would not have been surprised to know that his deputy did go upstairs to check the young girl's bedroom and that it was a *fruitless search. The house was left to its own silence: the front and back doors were boarded up, as were the windows. If the girl returned from visiting a friend she could be intercepted without even crossing the threshold. Arrangements were quickly made for her mother to be taken to the Service Laboratory for scanning and post-mortem examination. She was not the one they had wanted; her examination and compulsory yearly re-examination had revealed nothing unusual, no particularly advanced intellect, no particularly unusual elevation rating. She had always appeared 'normal' in all aspects. But Silva knew differently. Tania's mother had the capacity to block all known tests. She was, or had been, a very dangerous yet alluring woman.*

A skeletal surveillance team was positioned in an empty apartment across the road from the back of the house; in fact it had already been there for a number of months checking the movements of Tania's mother. This was upon Silva's insistence despite all the negative results from all her Elevation Tests. He wanted to know her every move. Why had she left the house so often? Where did she go?

He suspected that Nina Temple had been making arrangements for her daughter to disappear and possibly be cared for in a safe house out of view from drones and Security Patrols. The authorities were gradually finding these safe havens but it was a slow process thwarted by further surreptitious activity from the well organised rebels undermining governmental control. The early raid on the house had not given her enough time to secure an escape for Tania, but somehow or other she seemed to have eluded them without her mother's help.

A second team of observers sat in a Service Surveillance Vehicle at the end of the road in front of the house, at the exact same spot where Silva used to stand by the corner lamp. They were sure the girl would return soon. They were wrong.

Alone

The panelling on the stairway had held firm. Tania could only just decipher the muffled shouts from the rest of the house. Every clumsy thump from the searching servicemen reverberated through the whole building and still the panelling held firm, just as her mother had said it would. She was alone in the darkness and she dare not move. She knew that no one would hear her; she trusted every word her mother had said, but she could not take that risk just yet. She curled up in the cupboard, for that is all it was: a cupboard. It was a cupboard built for a purpose. It was a cupboard built to be a secret: fully insulated and fully kitted out for at least a month's survival. There were plenty of Meal Tablets, air-tight and fully labelled; sealed drinks; a pile of clothes; a torch, spare batteries and matches just in case; a knife and scissors; books, paper and pens. But there was no one to talk to; no one to confide in; and no one to embrace and be told that everything was going to be all right.

Her mother had been meticulous in the preparation of this hideout, in the same way she was meticulous in all she did. Tania had often wondered if it was this undying desire for everything to be perfect that played on her mother's nerves, for her mother was without doubt of an extremely nervous disposition. Or perhaps it was this highly-strung disposition that caused her to be extremely organised, knowing that imperfections would cause her edginess to become uncontrolled and uncontrollable.

Tania knew that if anyone had attacked her mother, she would have screamed. Why didn't she scream? Surely she would have had time to scream? Unless the assailant had come from behind, but even then her mother would have sensed the approach. Not only that, the door to the outside world was always locked; again, her mother made certain of this as she would never leave the door unlocked even for a few seconds. No one would have entered the house without her mother's knowledge. This led her to consider two possible options: her mother had known the assailant and opened the door to him or she had taken her own life. Considering the fact that the door had been smashed down, it was the latter option that seemed to be the more feasible. She did not want to linger on this possibility and consciously turned her thoughts to herself. She had to think about herself now.

How long could she stay in this confined space without venturing back into the house? How long would these intruders remain outside, waiting for her expected return? She knew that the apartment would be watched and she had to survive long enough for the authorities to lose interest and then she could leave and make her way to her mother's friend and hopefully to her own ultimate safety.

May Kilman

In the Couples Sector, a number of blocks away, stood a woman also suffering feelings of confinement. She was a woman who to all outward appearances had all she wanted: a beautiful apartment; stunning clothes; a young, ambitious husband who possessed a very high status post in the Government. She was, indeed, the focus of female envy from some quarters, but what did they know? In reality, she was an extremely troubled woman who considered herself to be equally as captive as Tania but for very different reasons. May Kilman leaned on the back of a chair in the middle of her immaculate kitchen. She was tired; a deep seated fatigue wracked her whole body and soul.

Mrs Kilman was in her late thirties yet looked ten years older. Like her kitchen, her outward appearance was immaculate but superficial. There was the flawless facial make-up; the impeccably manicured purple nails; the short hair-cut shaped around the nape of the neck that was the latest fashion, but no amount of cosmetic beautification and hair styling could hide the ravages of an unhappy life. Yet, despite all of this, May Kilman had not given up hope and that is why she persevered.

She looked around the room. Everything was clean; everything was in its place. What could he find fault with this time? She hoped it had been a good day for him. Her hand moved intuitively to her face; the swelling had started to subside and the violent purple bruising had turned to an ugly shade of muted jaundiced yellow, but she had powdered her face as always, for appearance's sake.

Kilman had been furious when that girl had disappeared. He had stomped angrily around the house, muttering about it all being a waste of precious time, that it was a set up and Silva had something to do with it all but he didn't know what. Her husband never totally confided in her; he said she wouldn't understand. But she understood enough to know that if things didn't go well, she was the one who would suffer and the suffering would often be of a physical nature.

There had been no news of the girl since the day she disappeared after the raid, two weeks previously. But there was something more; something eating away at Kilman. And his wife, as always, bore the brunt of his anger.

Cook a lovely dinner. That would help. She visited the Central Food Station that morning. There were two main options for the purchase of food in the township: fresh vegetables for home cooking or Meal Tablets which involved no cooking but were made up of all the nutrients needed for a healthy life (or so people were led to believe). These Meal Tablets varied in size ranging from that of a drawing pin head to that of a computer keyboard and were consumed in conjunction with a drink of water or cordial. Few citizens could afford alcohol and there were stringent restrictions in place regarding the amount that could be purchased.

Mrs Kilman had seen Silva in the Food Station heading directly to the area where the Meal Tablets were sold: no fussing about and time wasting for him in his approach to food it would seem. He certainly looked healthy enough but she did wonder about the long term effects of eating in this way, if indeed this was his eating practice of choice. The Tablets could be warmed up, but she doubted that the mindset of those who purchased them regularly was such that they would do this. She could not help but question, silently of course, what chemical additives were in them. Silva did not have to queue for a Courtesy Assistant to attend to his needs; his high office in the Government allowed him preferential treatment. However, like everyone else he did have to use the Food Station's Courtesy Assistants; he was not permitted to shop alone.

All items for sale in the Food Station were labelled with a computer chip that would react to the touch of a human hand. If anyone tried to handle any of the food products, be it a vegetable or a Meal Tablet, an alarm would be initiated. To avoid this occurring, every customer in the station was allocated a Courtesy Assistant who would walk around the Station with the customer and would use a metallic hand gadget to pick up the item requested by that customer. In recent months, androids had been introduced to do this work, thus avoiding the need for the Food Station to purchase extra hand gadgets or, indeed, pay for human Courtesy Assistants. Androids did not cost anything, and could be

71

placed into store cupboards during the night where their energy supplies could be recharged.

The purchased food item would be placed in the trolley which had to be pushed by the customer, thus, in theory at least, any form of shoplifting would be avoided. When the assistant had placed all of the items required by the customer into the trolley, it had to be pushed to the checkout. Once all items were paid for and placed in a Government Issue Holdall, the customer would walk through a security exit which would react with an alarm if any item had not been paid for or had not had its computer chip removed at the checkout.

May Kilman's preference for sustenance, unlike that of Silva apparently, was to make her way to the vegetable area. She already had the extra virgin oil, garlic and chilli powder at home but needed to get some onions, a couple of peppers, carrots and some herbs: coriander and cumin would be ideal. It was interesting to note that the predominant gender of the shoppers in the vegetable area was female and the predominant gender of the shoppers in the Meal Tablet area was male. She was not surprised by the image this portrayed of the society in which she lived.

Having collected her shopping, her allocated Shopping Assistant for the day escorted her out of the building and she started to make her way home. Suddenly she heard the distinctive authoritarian voice of a security air-drone.

"Halt! I order you in the name of The Government to stop immediately."

Everyone in the vicinity, except one man, stopped immediately as ordered. The man, probably in his late twenties, continued to run: Government Issue Holdall clutched closely to his chest.

The air-drone swiftly flew with ease over people and over vehicles; not one obstacle hindered the rapid pursuit. The man did not have a chance.

The air-drone soon caught up with him, overtook him and kept pace a couple of metres in front of him. "This is your final warning. You are to stop in the name of the Lithport Government."

The man slowed his pace and he came to a stop. His shoulders dropped and he looked towards the ground at his feet, submitting himself in meek acquiescence to the inevitable.

"Put the bag down. You have two options. Raise your right

72

arm for immediate disciplinary action; raise your left arm for a future Court of Justice hearing."

Every single human being within the area looked towards the man in shock, in fear, in sympathy, in relief that he and not they faced this travesty. Palpable silence embraced every soul. No one dare speak; no one dare breathe.

The man raised his head and looked in defiance at the inanimate judge hovering before him. He slowly raised his right arm.

Disciplinary action was, indeed, immediate. He fell forward onto his knees and his body slowly crumpled; his head touched the ground as he stooped in lifeless penitence. The contents of the Government Issue Holdall spilled over the walkway: fruit, vegetables, everyday items for which a man had given his life.

No one moved. The quiet whirring of the air-drone was all that could be heard. Within a few moments a Government vehicle arrived and swept the inert body into its belly. Then life began again as if nothing had happened.

May Kilman walked home.

Spicy vegetable chilli, his favourite meal, was simmering quietly on the hob. The occasional pop of the sauce was somehow comforting to her. This was one meal she knew she could not spoil, however late home he might be. When she put it on the table she would garnish it with a fresh coriander sprig. She also had his favourite crusty loaf, newly warmed in the oven. Why did she do this just for him? Despite everything she had to endure, why was there still this deep affection for him? This need to please him?

The door to the kitchen slid open with a sibilant whisper. Kilman strode into the room. There was no acknowledgement of his wife's presence. Well, being ignored was better than being hit. She still made an effort. "Hello love."

Kilman muttered something inarticulate. He left the room and within minutes he returned minus his coat and folder of papers. He sat at the table like a lord in dominion over all of his surroundings. He was ready to be served.

May placed a mug of warm lemon tea in front of him. She gently pushed the switch for the wall screen to activate and pressed the repeat button for the official news broadcast she had

d

heard earlier. She hoped that the news would be welcomed by her husband. The loud automated and authoritative voice burst upon them, "The so called safe house in The Eastern Province has now been fully demolished."

She paused, waiting for a reaction. Perhaps her husband, in his workplace capacity, had already heard this sound-bite, but she added the extra information that had been made public when she listened to the airing on her return from the Food Station, "Three bodies were found. I don't think they've been identified yet. Two of them were children." The Eastern Province was two streets away from where the missing girl had lived and it was possible that she had been visiting a friend there. May thought this might be good news for Kilman, but he was probably already aware of it and she knew better than to ask him what sort of day he had had.

He was clearly not even listening, so she switched off the screen, although if the authorities had news they wanted the citizens to hear they would override the workings of the screen at any time. The essential broadcast would be relayed in all apartments and in the streets.

Kilman stared ahead and, without even looking at her, asked abruptly, "How old are you?"

"Thirty-nine. You know I'm thirty-nine." As soon as she had said this, she regretted the added comment. Did he really not know his own wife's age?

"If I knew I wouldn't have asked." He slurped his tea slowly and loudly. Five years or more ago, she would have lightly reprimanded him, but not now. "Your brother's twelve years older than you, isn't he? He was in the same academic training year as Silva, wasn't he? Did he ever talk about him? What was he like at the academy? Was he clever?"

Kilman spat the questions out like bullets from the stomach of an automaton machine gun. May wondered what had started this interrogation. He rarely mentioned his senior officer, until recently, and even then not directly to her; he muttered his name, or what sounded like his name, over and over again in his sleep. She never told her husband that he talked in his sleep. She wondered now what was really on his mind. She didn't trust him. The thought that she didn't trust her own husband truly scared her.

"I don't think my brother was one of his friends. They didn't really know each other that well. They didn't associate with each other very much."

"They didn't associate with each other very much." He deliberately stressed the final two words and looked at her with his piercing blue eyes: eyes in which she had to admit that she had lost herself all those years ago. "What do you mean by 'very much'?"

May needed to be careful. Her brother had known Silva; in fact, he had known him very well. Everyone knew Silva. Silva was academic, sporty, handsome and very popular with everyone, male and female: fellow students and tutors alike. He had everything and everyone knew he would do well in life. He held the respect of peers and academy trainers. Whereas her husband, seventeen years Silva's junior, got what he wanted through aggression and family status. He was, in short, a bully.

So, why had she married him? She did not love him with that heart stopping desire to be with him every moment of every day and never had; and yet there was a deep attraction. There was an inner unwavering belief that beyond the outer bravado was something genuine; there was a man who wanted everyone to feel that there was something worth living for, that life could work for everyone. You do not marry someone because they have piercing blue eyes. But, she had known love: true, unselfish, all-consuming love. Paul Ryan was a beautiful young man who had been attacked and killed one night after walking her home: attacked for no discernible reason other than a few brexemes and a wrist-watch. Kilman was the leading officer. He found the two culprits. He dealt with them swiftly. He had seen that justice was done. She was grateful. But you do not marry someone merely because you are grateful.

She nervously twisted the unpretentious wedding band round and round and round her finger. She knew that she would have married that beautiful young man, but he was gone. Nevertheless, she had no regrets: something was truly eating away at Kilman and she wanted to understand what it was. There was an inner conflict and she would help him through it.

Kilman needed a wife. He was not entirely sure that he wanted a wife; he simply needed a wife. A wife would bring prestige and acceptability in the establishment. It would also ensure an *apartment in the Couple Sector. Courting was far too tedious for him; love was a whimsical emotion and he was not a whimsical man. May Puerto was just right: a woman who was possibly too old to find a new suitor. She had had her romance and now she would be grateful that someone would show interest in her; he was not concerned that she was five years his senior. What did that matter? It would be a marriage of convenience to all concerned. It was an ideal arrangement.*

May Puerto and Warren Kilman were married within a month of meeting each other. May Puerto was no more; she was now May Kilman and part of the establishment. Women were not permitted to retain their surname when married; that privilege had long disappeared.

Alone No Longer

After a few days cooped up in the confinement of the stairwell cupboard, Tania felt brave enough to venture into the emptiness of the house. She knew no one was there. There was no presence and she suspected that the inevitable surveillance outside the building would also soon be gone.

It did not matter that the whole house was plunged into an eerie blackness; she knew every single centimetre of every single room. She did not even need to use the torch. She just needed to stretch her young muscles.

Her initial forays were brief: a quick visit to the bathroom; a return to her bedroom to pick up personal items such as her musical ballerina, a small rag doll and some hair accessories. There was no point in tidying up the mess that the Government official had created in his angry fruitless search for her. She pulled her hair back and tied it with a lovely pink ribbon; it was a small gesture but it made her feel happy. On each trip she always ensured that she stepped over the third stair; perhaps its inevitable creak was too poignant a reminder of the fateful day she lost her mother.

They had taken her mother away. She had not had the opportunity to say her final goodbye. Her mother had warned her that this might happen, but she never truly believed that it would. What was the last conversation they had had? She remembered the two of them sitting together for dinner and Tania had taken

76

the final dose of medicine; medicine that would screen her inner being; medicine that would hide her true empathies; medicine that would fool the machine into believing that she was not an Elevationist and not in possession of too high an intelligence quotient. What sacrifices her mother must have made to be able to afford such a powerful drug. She suspected that her mother's friend, who worked in the governmental laboratories, had something to do with their access to the medicine, but she did not ask any awkward questions.

Her mother told her that she had a gift. She had a gift of which she should be proud: femininity and sensitivity that no man would ever understand.

Tania counted the days following her mother's death. She recorded each as accurately as she could on the wall of the cupboard: a single downward pen line for each day. She wrote her thoughts in the empty book her mother had left her. A potent sense of loneliness invaded her soul, but she was determined that her spirit for survival would not be shaken by negative thoughts. Images of her mother served to strengthen her resolve.

She had to be brave, not in the sense of sacrificing her life and giving up everything she had known for some great cause. She just had to get through the pain and manage her daily existence; whatever that entailed. This was the bravery she needed to embrace.

She read illicit novel after illicit novel until tiredness had forced her into uncomfortable slumber. Two weeks passed and she knew that she must soon venture forth into the world and find her mother's friend whom she affectionately referred to as aunt. After a month of emptiness any household would be demolished to make way for a new property. Demolition would rid an old building of any evil, any sign of who had been there before.

Then one evening, she felt his presence. She knew it was the man from the street corner. He had been in the group of men that had raided her home. Had he been the one who had killed her mother? She was sure he hadn't. She realised that he was back here to look for her before the whole house was due for demolition. She heard a voice that she had heard before and her name being called, just as on that fateful evening. "Tania?"

She did not answer.

His voice was soft, "I know you are still here, Tania. And I know you don't want to speak with me. Perhaps you think I killed your mother, but I did not." She could feel sincerity in his tone, in his inner mind, but she did not, could not, trust him. Perhaps he also took medicine to block his inner feelings. "I want to help you to escape. You have nowhere to go. The Eastern Province safe house has been destroyed."

How did he know about the Eastern Province? Was he speaking the truth? She searched in his mind for some sign of deceit, for a mask shielding the truth of his inner self. There were shadows, but she could not fully detect their meaning.

She slowly descended the stairs. He held a torch, its light directed towards the floor so as not to blind her. She could make out his outline and she knew that he was, indeed, the man with the trilby hat; the wearer of the black gabardine; the cigarette smoker. And finally she would speak with him but not under the circumstances for which she had originally hoped.

Silva looked up to see the silhouette of a small fragile figure. "Hello Tania."

She was surprised that he knew her name, but she also knew his name; he did not hold any advantage over her in this, so she acknowledged his greeting. "Hello Mr Silva."

He was also surprised. He had not expected her mother to have told her about him. He wondered how much she knew.

Tania slowly descended the stairwell. She could still not see him clearly, but she didn't need to. She felt safe for the moment.

"We have to get away, Tania, before they destroy your home with you in it. The surveillance teams have gone now; they have assumed that you are not returning; that you are dead or somehow beyond their reach."

Tania knew that if she herself wanted something, if she really wanted something, she would not give up, she would continue looking, searching and digging away. But perhaps these people did not want her that much. She couldn't understand why they should anyway. She was just a girl, an ordinary girl. She didn't really feel that she had a special gift. But it seemed that she had no choice; she would go with this man. She had no one else now.

Kilman

Kilman could not help but wonder why he treated May in this barbaric way. He was so engrossed in his work; it was his whole life. It was the reason he existed. There was nothing else. He knew that he did not actually love her; however, he could at least treat her with some degree of respect. She deserved no less than this. But there were the headaches. He could feel their onset. He had always been prone to headaches, even as a child, but these recent ones had hammered his head remorselessly. He tried to ignore them. He tried to extricate himself from all around him when he felt the quiet but insistent surge that he knew would lead to the blinding pain, the unyielding thumping. He wanted to scream, but what did he do? He hit out, and his wife was the one who suffered. The headaches were always worse at home than at work. In fact, the headaches invariably occurred at home, when he tried to relax, when he tried to let the concerns of the day dissipate.

He started to wonder if his wife was slowly poisoning him. He wouldn't blame her. He was becoming neurotic: he started to insist that he made his own drinks; he checked the ingredients in all the food cupboards. There was no way that she could understand all the pressure that he was under.

Perhaps his continued exposure to various chemicals in the laboratories was having an effect. He even toyed with the idea of suffering from dementia but he had no memory loss; he was extremely well organised; he did not become easily confused, yet there were definite mood swings and anxiety. He dismissed his thoughts as ridiculous, but something was wrong and he wanted to know what it was.

However, he knew that he held a personal secret: a secret that had the potential to destroy his status as an upright citizen. He had to be careful.

An Empathetic Relationship?

The large black leather seat embraced Tania as she sat beside Silva who eased his company limousine smoothly through the streets of Lithport. She had to strain her neck to tentatively look out upon the houses, the people, the fitness clinics, the huge Food Stations. Silva felt her hesitancy. "Don't worry. No one can see into the car. We can see out of the blackened windows, but no one can see in."

"Why did you kill my mother, Mr Silva?"

Silva was momentarily stunned by the sudden abruptness of this young girl. However, he answered calmly and, indeed, truthfully for he was not the one who had actually brought about the end of her mother's life, "I didn't kill your mother."

"But you are responsible for my mother's death even if you didn't actually kill her yourself." Her understanding was unequivocal.

"I tried to save her. That is why I ran across the road to your apartment, but I was too late." He did not expand upon why he had actually wanted to save her: why he had wanted to see the look of desperate understanding on her face as he took her daughter from her, leaving her utterly alone.

"You knew that we were going to be raided. Why didn't you warn us? Why didn't you warn me? You could have warned me. Did you want her to die, Mr Silva?"

"I did not want her to die, Tania. She was once a good friend. I wanted to save her life."

There was that significant word again: once.

"You are the head of security aren't you? You would be the one who arranged the raid. You killed my mother." Her logic was impeccable and not exactly inaccurate either.

He was stunned by her perception and understanding. "You are almost twelve years old. You knew that it was time for your Elevation Test. I am sure that your mother had told you about it."

"But not in that way and not yet. You came early, Mr Silva. My mother was not expecting you that early. Normally the mother takes the child to the laboratories herself and is given the opportunity to say goodbye. Not many mothers deliberately avoid this by trying to escape as they know that they will be hunted down. My mother would have taken me at the allocated time. Why was she not given the opportunity to say goodbye to me?"

How much had her mother told her?

"Yes, I did arrange the raid. I have to remain in my position as Head of Government and Societal Communication in order that I can help more people. I hope you will soon fully understand. I have to be seen to be doing my job. Sometimes this means that I have to spring surprises, surprises that I hope will not have . . ."

He hesitated, ". . . awful consequences. I thought that I could get to your mother before Mr Kilman, my deputy. It wasn't your mother he wanted. I didn't think he would take any notice of her."

Silva was falsifying facts and wondered whether Tania could detect his lying, but she seemed to be focused on continuing to ask her questions and perhaps not fully concentrating on the answers given, or not on the possible disingenuous nature of the answers given. Perhaps no one had ever lied to her before.

"No. It was me he wanted. And your deputy is the type of man who will get rid of anyone in his way and it was obvious that my mother would get in his way. Why did he want me so badly, Mr Silva?"

Her deceptively polite Mr Silva was beginning to irk him, but he remained calm. "You have a gift. You have a gift that is invaluable, beautiful even, but you have a gift that Kilman is afraid of. He doesn't understand anyone who doesn't fit what he sees as being normal. He wants to eradicate anything he sees as being abnormal or different."

Her mother had told her that she had a gift. Stressing the first syllable of her next question, she asked, "Am I abnormal, Mr Silva?"

"No. You have a gift."

"So have you." He didn't expect this response.

"No. Not in the same way you have." Silva was not a natural Elevationist; after all, he was a man, how could he be an Elevationist? However, he had learned not exactly to control his mind, but to temporarily deflect an Elevationist's inquisitorial thoughts. Tania wondered if he had taken drugs like she had done, but to help him read people's thoughts as opposed to taking drugs intended to mask a 'gift'.

He could not tell if Tania trusted him yet. He wanted her to trust him. At this moment in time, he felt that he needed her trust. "You know we have something in common, you and I. My number at the Institute when I was your age was 48, just like yours. It was 48R because of my first name, but I think that you and I were destined to meet."

Tania said nothing. She knew that he was avoiding sensitive areas of discussion. She deliberately did not ask what the letter R signified.

Silva decided to try again. "In some small way I think that I can give you the opportunity to say goodbye to your mother."

"How?"

"I have kept her ashes securely locked up in my office so that you can scatter them wherever you wish and say your own personal goodbye. It may be a poor substitute but it might help."

There was no reply. The subject was not pursued further at this time. Silence held dominion.

Within minutes, they had arrived at the Security Station: an ugly grey building of four storeys in height, symmetrical in appearance with windows that looked like a thousand eyes sneering at the tiny vulnerable child. Tania was suddenly afraid. This was not where she wanted to be. This was where they held the Test. Had Silva fooled her? He had told her that they were going to The Wall and beyond, and she had mentally prepared herself for this.

"Please don't be afraid. It may seem odd but this is the safest place for you because this is the last place that anyone will think to look for you. And we are not actually going to enter the main building."

The barrier rose smoothly and then came to a juddering halt at the pinnacle. Silva drove beneath the wavering arm before it descended again behind them.

"Remember, no one can see into the car. It will be assumed that I am on my own. My car was recognised and that is why the barrier lifted."

"Anybody could be driving your car." This was yet another very simple but highly observant comment from the young girl.

"The car recognises the driver. Only I can drive this car. It would not function for anybody else. Not even an android. The internal computer workings have this capability within all of our vehicles. Each vehicle is programmed to function for one person and will not move for anyone else. In fact, an alarm would be set off if anyone tried to hijack a vehicle and if the thief did manage to get in to the vehicle, he or she would be locked inside as there is an automatic locking system in place."

Tania seemed satisfied with this response and he followed the driveway towards the Security Station and then took a left fork when it divided into two. He manoeuvred the car around the huge building that dominated the lives of those who lived in the confines of Lithport and drove beyond, towards another building which was smaller but still had the clinical look of officialdom.

"What is that building?"

Silva showed no emotion either in his tone of voice or his facial expression, "It's called The Crematorium." He knew it was not a place where people were cremated, but a transitional waiting area for girls who had scored too highly in the Elevation Test. He was interested in Tania's response.

She did not, however, respond verbally. Inside she could not help but wonder if he was going to kill her and put her body in The Crematorium, yet she knew better than to voice her concerns. In times of doubt, it was best not to say anything.

"I have to make regular checks there. Remember, I am in charge of this whole procedure."

He slowed the car to a halt and parked to the side of the large shed-like building. The vehicle's central locking system clicked and the doors opened automatically. They alighted. "We should go in this way." Tania followed Silva towards the building. He pointed to a door at the back to which they made their way and then went through. Tania was surprised by what she saw. She expected to smell the scent of death, to feel the heat of demonic flames, to be overwhelmed, but she wasn't. They walked along corridor after corridor; but she knew that she could find her way back again if necessary. They passed by many doors until finally leaving behind what was seemingly the last one, they proceeded towards a wall.

"Have you ever read the book about a boy called Harry Potter, who was a magician or wizard or something like that?"

Was he testing her? Books and films about the occult and all other fictional material had been banned many years before. "Yes, Mr Silva, I've read all of the Harry Potter books." There seemed little point in denying the truth.

Silva smiled. "I thought you might have done." He paused. "Well, we are just going to walk right through this wall." He put his flat palm facing upwards onto a small area of the wall and a door-sized section slid open in front of them both. He then put his palm back onto the exact place and the section closed. "You try." She did so and the section opened again. He turned and looked her in the eye, "Just like your panelling at home, I believe. Only the panelling at your home would only respond to your hand print." She had not told him about the panelling to the cupboard. How did he know about it? If truth be told, it was actually what might be described as an *intelligent guess on his part. She tried to reach into his mind, but there was nothing.*

"At first I wanted the opening to the passageway to respond to only my hand print but I realised that no one would ever come this way so it seemed an unnecessary extravagance." It did not take an Elevationist to recognise the confidence, verging on arrogance, in his demeanour.

"Follow me." Silva walked ahead of her and she followed. She had to trust this man; she had no choice. For the moment, she had to do exactly what he said.

"We are now on the other side of The Wall."

"The wall of a building or The Wall separating us from the wasteland beyond our township?" She asked.

"The Wall separating us from the wasteland beyond our township. No building wall is that tall." There was a playfulness in his voice.

Tania wondered if he was mocking her but everything around suddenly felt totally overwhelming. The scene that met her eyes was stunning. It was as if they had stepped into another world, which in many respects they had: an alien world. No one ventured beyond The Wall if they wanted to live. This is where wild creatures roamed unchecked. This is where there was no control over the weather. She felt light droplets of water falling from above and trickling down her neck.

Silva laughed quietly at her confused response. "Natural rain: a much different texture than you are used to in Lithport. It can get much harder than this sometimes. It can soak you within seconds, but it is far more refreshing than the chemical liquid substance that falls on you within The Wall. You'll get used to it. You wait until you experience real snow. That's exciting. It covers everything in a carpet of pure white. It is soft to the touch; not like our artificial stuff."

Tania found this hard to imagine, but she desperately tried to pull her mind away from all that lay in front of her and concentrate on the man standing at her side. His mind was a series of shadows again. This unnerved her. Sometimes she could feel him but sometimes he seemed to close himself off from her. No one had ever been able to do that before.

Chapter Five

A Fortuitous Spillage

It was time for a welcome comfort stop before cracking on. While she waited for the kettle to boil, Myra paid a brief visit to the bathroom. A quick freshen up was in order. No facial cosmetics were needed today; just a splash of cold water on the face would do the trick. Making sure that she did not dwell on her reflection in the mirror, she perused her bathroom cabinet for the refreshing facial wash that would help her to feel more invigorated, even if her outward appearance belied this sense of well-being.

The tools of the feminal trade waited in readiness before her on the shelf: hair shampoo, hair conditioner, shower gel, body lotion, body spray, hair colouring and various items of make-up. Her wonderful bag of tricks working together as one to help provide her female empowerment.

She reached across towards the bright orange spray can standing sentinel at the back of the cabinet, propping up the ladies' razor that had seen better days and really needed to be replaced. Ladies' Hair Removal Mousse: 'helps your skin feel smoother for longer' with its 'new, improved texture'. She looked at the extensive list of ingredients: so many for one small can. And such an innocent name for a beauty product: mousse. It sounded good enough to eat and yet what damage all those ingredients could do if inwardly digested instead of massaged into the skin: potassium thioglycolate, sodium hydroxide, propane, isobutane, cetearyl alcohol, sodium silicate, petrolatum, carbomer, hexamethyldisiloxane, paraffin, prunus amygdalus dulcis oil, sodium gluconate, butylene glycol. The list seemed endless and totally incomprehensible.

What would happen if just one of these ingredients were to be removed or replaced with something else? What power could be engendered across the whole country if every can of Ladies' Hair Removal Mousse in the factories across the land had been doctored to some small degree.

Myra smiled. Her imagination was running away with her yet again.

She reached across to replace the can and in so doing knocked her arm against the hair shampoo. It rocked very gently for a moment before falling against other products until the ultimate victim of the domino effect was a small plum-red bottle of perfume: 'Amor Amor'. It fell to the floor and smashed; its liquid contents flowed onto the tiling.

"Oh shit!"

She decided that the mess could just stay where it was for now; she would clear it up later. She had a more important task to carry out. Fortunately the noisy diversion had not disturbed Miriam, but had once again instilled more ideas in her head.

Collecting her cup of coffee from the kitchen, she returned to her study.

Myra's Manuscript Notes:

The laboratory
Drug tampering
A warning

Fiction

The Manuscript
Part Five

Lisa Watts

Tania's mother did not have to die. Why had Silva brought forward the raid? And the question that was most worrying of all to Lisa at this moment was: why had he not told her? She thought that they had built up a strong relationship; she needed him to feel able to confide in her. Tania's Elevation Examination was not due for at least another two weeks. Something or someone had spooked Silva and she wanted to know the culprit.

Nina Alexander had been a true friend; in fact, the two of them had been so close over the years that they thought of each other as family and Tania actually called her Aunt Lisa. Tania's shadowing course was not fully complete. Lisa did not know if the young girl would be able to mask her skills. But what did it matter now? She had disappeared. Lisa wondered if Silva actually knew where the girl was. She strongly suspected that he did.

A hint of nostalgia caused her to think about the time when Tania had asked her if she really was her mother's sister. She thought that sisters were supposed to look alike and they did not look anything like each other. The adamant and matter of fact way in which the young girl stated this made them both laugh. Lisa told her that although they were not blood relatives, they were extremely close: kindred spirits. Of course, she then had to go on and explain to Tania what a kindred spirit was and that in times gone past, her mother would have wanted her to be Tania's godparent. Tania's insatiable appetite for knowledge meant that *she almost demanded to know what a godparent actually was and what it meant to be a godparent as she was not familiar with the term.*

Lisa explained that many years ago, when people were permitted to have a divine belief in an almighty controlling power, there were a number of religions that people followed to guide them through life. One very popular religion, known as Christianity, centred on God the creator and ruler of the universe and source of all moral authority.

"A bit like the Government?" asked Tania.

Lisa had smiled at this. "No, nothing like the Government. People wanted to follow God and his teachings. Sometimes we don't always want to follow the Government and their demands. And, contrary to general belief, the Government are not almighty or superhuman even if they believe they are."

She went on to explain that it was an honour for a person to be asked to be a child's godparent. A godparent's role was to stay connected with the child in some manner throughout life and hopefully be an integral part of the child's spiritual upbringing. Sadly, spirituality did not form the basis of today's society. She made it very clear that Tania was not to speak about this to anyone and she knew that Tania would comply with that request, realising even at such an early age how fraught with danger all their lives were. Tania would, however, continue to call her Aunt Lisa.

Lisa Watts was so entirely embraced by her reverie that she had not noticed the forlorn figure and her daughter standing nervously at the crossways where the automobile lanes converged and branched off in four different directions.

The destination for the township's driverless vehicles needed to be programmed at the beginning of any specific journey in order to successfully negotiate the lane changes. In reality it was a feature of twenty-fourth century driving that was often ignored by a number of vehicle owners: perhaps they wanted to change their destination part of the way through the journey and it was too much of a hassle to alter the original programming. Or perhaps they wanted to feel the sense of power engendered by actually driving the car without the aid of a computer. Apparently some people actually enjoyed driving, although Lisa could not comprehend this attitude at all. Whatever the reason, if there was to be any vehicular mishap or accident, this was the likely place for it to occur. Many automobile owners could not be described as having the road sense that was brought about by frequent driving and familiarity with the automobile lanes; their ineptitude was what had necessitated a recent ruling that all vehicle owners should use the driverless facility in their cars, and yet it was a policy that many chose to ignore.

With regard to this particular junction, two or more automobiles frequently converged at once. If the owners had little experience of driving, it was reasonably inevitable that a collision could take place despite the advances in technology that, in theory at least, should ensure that any contact would not occur.

Being found guilty of ignoring the recent ruling concerning the compulsory driverless facility brought about a warning and possibly a correction course. Neither of these penalties had proved to be a deterrent. Lisa suspected that the disciplinary action would soon become far more severe.

Suddenly, without warning, there was a deafening screech of grinding metal. The girl on the pathway screamed and the older woman lay motionless in the automobile lane. Lisa stopped momentarily and soon realised that there were many people converging on the scene and her presence would do nothing to help the situation. Being focused on other matters that concerned the welfare of a different child was imperative for her at this time. As sad as she felt for the woman and the girl, their future was in the hands of others. Men emerged from vehicles, people stood at the side of the lanes. There was blaming and counter-blaming but the fact remained that yet another human being had clearly been determined to take her own life. There were so many reasons that could have brought about this unquenchable resolve.

Lisa quickened her pace. The artificial daylight was weakening and although the likelihood of attack was so minimal since the increase of Servicemen Patrols, she never enjoyed the walk to the laboratory when she was on a late shift. Furthermore, the suicide, for that is what she had just witnessed, would attract people's attention for a while. However, she did not want to be behind time. Since taking over some of Silva's duties, his deputy Kilman had sacked a number of workers recently for seemingly trivial misdemeanours. Lisa needed this post; so many young lives depended on her. Perhaps Nina Alexander's death had been partly her responsibility; she felt a tinge of guilt. Could she have done more to help?

Within a few moments she had arrived at her destination.

"Okay Lisa?" The security guard waved her through before she had even fully shown her card. And did he actually wink at her? Tom had been the security guard at the entrance barrier for as long as she could remember. Wisps of greying hair stuck out from underneath his uniform cap, but this was the only sign of individuality that he allowed himself as his appearance was always pristine. Lisa could visualise him routinely hanging the suit in a plastic bag after ensuring that he had brushed any loose hairs from the shoulders and collar. He would have the uniform cleaned every week without fail and he would thoroughly polish his shoes each morning ready for the evening shift. He took such pride in all he did.

But Tom needed to be more careful, she thought, as Kilman would not tolerate any lapse in vigilance. She walked towards the Security Station and up to her laboratory. She wondered who was on duty with her this evening. She normally ensured that she was fully aware of everyone on duty; but the death of Tania's mother had unnerved her. She needed to snap out of this. She reminded herself again: so many young lives depended on her actions.

Before entering the laboratory, she checked the charts outside to see if there were any Tests in the diary. Just as expected, there were none. When she entered the room, all was silent, but she was surprised to see a large black office swivel chair blocking the way to the benches. Within seconds it spun around and she came face to face with the stony stare of Kilman.

"Good evening Ms Watts." He did not wait for a response. "I see that there are no Tests this evening. What exactly do you do when there are no Elevation Tests, Ms Watts?" He spat out the word 'Ms' as if it was a bad taste in his mouth.

She was briefly taken aback, but soon recovered.

"I check all the machinery. I also check the balance of the truth telling drugs for the Elevation Test. I ensure the staffing rota is fair and . . ."

"Fair?" Kilman interrupted her. "What do you mean by fair?"

"That the hours are equal." He did not reply and so, for some reason, she felt compelled to add a hurried "Sir."

"The hours should be the same, day in day out, so that everyone knows exactly when they are working and there is equality not fairness."

Lisa tried to justify her philosophy. "There may be times that certain people want to change their day or their hours. An illness for example."

The abrupt and uncompromising response was immediate, "There should be no exceptions."

It seemed pointless to state in her defence the obvious basic truth that people could not help but suffer illnesses on occasions.

Kilman insisted on seeing every cupboard, every shelf, every bottle. In short: everything. He ran his hands across each shelf and inspected his fingers as if to check for dust particles; scrutinised labels; turned bottles upside down and even shook some of them.

"What exactly does this do?" He held up the phial of bright green liquid that was used for each Test. Lisa could not for a moment believe that he did not recognise the truth telling drug used in the Elevation Test. Its distinct colour ensured its prominence over the rest of the other liquids in the laboratory innocently lining the walls that surrounded where the two of them now stood facing each other.

"It ensures that the examinee tells the truth and does not mask any information of which he or she is aware."

Then came the question that she had been dreading, "If such a drug as this exists, then there must be at least the potential for a drug that can mask the truth. Isn't that right?"

He was not an Elevationist; she knew this, yet she still paused, trying desperately to mask her thoughts.

"Well?" his voice rose threateningly.

"It's possible." Her voice was quiet but surprisingly calm and measured.

"Yes, it is possible, but to your knowledge does such a drug exist?"

She remained calm.

He repeated his question, deliberately pausing between each word and stressing every single syllable, "Does such a drug exist?"

"Poss. . ."

"Yes or no!" His raised voice reverberated around the room. Lisa could almost feel the glass phials huddling together on the shelving and shivering fearfully as if acknowledging their imminent danger. With one sweep of his arm, Kilman could destroy years of work. The bottles would fall, crashing down to the floor, shattering into countless tiny slivers of glass, their liquid contents freely flowing in rivulets across the floor. Plastic bottles, despite their imperishable quality, had proven to be unsuitable for such precious goods.

"No." Her economy of truth remained unblemished.

"And you know of no one who is working on producing such a drug?"

"No."

Kilman turned. She was safe. For the moment. Then he slowly twisted around again and, looking straight at her, called for the guards. The door immediately opened, but the people who arrived were not just guards, there were also laboratory experts: people she recognised, people with whom she had worked, people who looked very afraid. "Well. . ." his voice was unctuous; he was clearly confident in the knowledge that whatever she said, he would find out the truth, ". . .we are about to find out."

The system employed at the laboratory was very simple: all of the laboratory experts worked on a one in three week rota. They each had a team of assistants but it was the laboratory expert who was responsible each week for the drugs that were administered. The team worked from 8.00 in the morning until midday, had an hour break and then worked from 1.00 until 5.00 in the evening. No tests were administered from midday until 1.00 p.m. and during that time the laboratory was closed and locked. Only the laboratory experts, certain security guards and the senior team, in other words, Silva and Kilman, had keys. One of the laboratory experts stayed at work but was joined by the laboratory expert on evening duty – on this particular evening it

92

was Lisa. Both workers stayed until 8.00 p.m. to ensure that everything was prepared for the following day and, very occasionally, conduct more testing. They worked seven days per week: the outdated twentieth century idea of the weekend had not existed for many years. Each laboratory expert and his or her team worked from Monday through until Sunday.

Night shifts were generally supervisory and undertaken each evening during the week following the daytime duty. Guards were always present throughout the building, but an expert had to be on hand at all times. Laboratory supervisors were permitted to participate in drug research during this time as long as it benefited the 'system' and was documented in detail.

Lisa was totally aware that during her own working week all the bottles were accounted for. She was meticulous in this. But although all the bottles were accounted for, she was also fully aware that the colour of the solution she used was slightly different to that of the other narcohypnotic drugs. It was a very subtle difference and almost imperceptible, but placed next to an original Truth Testing solution, could be detected if scrutinised closely.

She felt quite confident that no one else in the laboratory was aware of this change. On a number of occasions she had deliberately used her powers of Elevation to probe the minds of her fellow laboratory experts.

The change of solution did not happen every evening of her working week; some weeks it did not happen at all but she knew that when it did, during the next day's testing no one was ever given a positive test result detecting dangerous traits of Elevation. It usually occurred when the young person being tested was female. On these days, not one young life was ever at risk; not one young person was identified as being an Elevationist. Surely that must be a good thing?

She had desperately hoped that Tania's test would be while she was on duty, but unfortunately she had had no influence regarding the recent premature raid. She no longer had any control over Tania's future, although she had managed to get some masking drugs to her in recent months.

Lisa had not told anyone about the changes in the truth telling drug. Young people's lives were being saved. Young girls in particular were being given a chance.

93

Yes she did worry that her data would not be compatible with the data of the other two weeks when she was not on duty. But so be it. She knew that one day there would be an investigation but she honestly had no idea who was changing the drugs. Each week she tested their authenticity and each week she knew that whoever was changing the drugs knew what he or she was doing: the quality was unquestionable.

She lived in this blessed ignorance until one evening she had to stay at the laboratory for longer than usual and in walked Silva. They did not need to say anything. He knew. She knew. From that day on her blessed ignorance was not quite so secure.

Whenever she met him in the corridor, she could not look him in the eye. Then one day, unexpectedly, he called her to his office. He talked about his wife; how she had been an Elevationist and how much he loved her but how she had died in childbirth and that there was no treatment that could have saved her. He also stated that the baby had died. He could not help but place some of the blame on the staff and androids for their lack of communication and incompetence. He felt that there were still so many illnesses for which there was no cure and yet the society in which they lived continued to insist on eliminating healthy young people. It was so wrong. What had become of their society that young lives were considered expendable?

She remembered the way he had looked directly at her, not accusatorily, but with a desire to understand. He wanted to know if she was responsible for the lower identification rate during her week on duty, and if not, whether she was aware of who was. She felt so confident, almost pleased with herself, when she said, "I do now." There was a pause and then they both smiled. She knew he was responsible; there was no one else it could be.

He conceded. He told Lisa that this was why in some minor way he tried to save some of these girls. It might only be a small recompense, a small victory, but it was something. Here was a beautiful, but lonely man. He sat in his office, day after day, the commander of a huge organisation and yet in some ways the prisoner of that organisation.

She wanted to reach out to him; to run her fingers through that beautiful dark hair that had begun to turn silver in places; to lose herself in those eyes; to totally yield herself to him. And she did. Not there and not then but they started to meet, sometimes at his

94

apartment, sometimes at her apartment. They went to concerts together. In fact, they had gone to one only a few evenings before. She fully understood how a woman could fall in love with this man. It took a huge strength of will not to do just that. Part of her believed that Tania's mother must have fallen for his undeniable charms.

"Ms Watts." Kilman's voice broke into and shattered Lisa's reverie. He then turned and announced to the whole room, "Well, everything seems to be in order here. You may all go." And with those few brief words, he dismissed all the personnel from the laboratory, until only the two of them stood looking directly at each other.

"Do not think I don't realise that there are issues here, Ms Watts. I will continue to closely monitor all the activities in this laboratory." Then, with a gentler timbre, he added, "Please be careful, Ms Watts, and do ensure that you remain professional at all times." The words were harsh and foreboding; the tone was calm and measured. He turned and left.

The room fell silent. Lisa's nerves were at breaking point. She needed to speak with Silva, but she had no idea where he was.

Reality

Chapter Six

A Walk in the Park

Myra did not usually let every day noises around her play on her nerves while she was fully focused on her writing. In fact, when she was fully focused on her writing she rarely let anything at all disturb her. However, today had become extremely frustrating. The seeming collusion of Miriam's incessant crying, her own lack of restful sleep, the arguing from the next apartment and the cacophonous sounds of the unusually busy amount of traffic outside, all combined to force her to rethink her morning's agenda.

It was a beautiful day: warm, dry, sunny. Yet it was still with some degree of reluctance that she decided she would take Miriam to the nearby park. The two of them made their way down the road: Miriam quietly burbling to herself in her own unfathomable baby language that only she could understand, and Myra wondering about how to move ahead with her manuscript. Her irritable mood was gradually dissipating into what many might describe as normality.

Parent and daughter made their way down the road, over the pedestrian crossing and past the ruins of a house that had recently suffered a gas explosion. Apparently three bodies were found in the crumbled remains of the building: two children below the age of five and an adult, believed to be their mother. Myra had read about it in the local newspaper; in fact, it had had some influence on her fictional trio of deaths in the Eastern Province safe house.

So yet again, reality had become her literary morphallaxis; fiction and reality merging into one. Myra did not know the unfortunate family and spent little time either thinking about them or the terrible circumstances that had brought about the untimely death of two youngsters who would never fulfil the aspects of life that many of us take for granted: school days, friendships, romantic relationships, marriage. Apparently the distraught grandparents had even scattered the family's ashes on this area of concrete devastation. It was strange to think of human remains mingling with bricks and mortar in a shared grave of filthy rubble as if the people and the building held parity.

Myra took Miriam down the lane towards the iron gates that heralded the entrance to the park. She manoeuvred the buggy round the two off-set gates and pushed her daughter over the pathway towards the play area where children laughed excitedly and screamed with nervous energy. Some shuffled tentatively down the slide while others careered headfirst at breakneck speed towards the unyielding ground beneath. Others ran round madly, missing by only a few centimetres the flailing legs of those on the swings. A little boy tottered unsteadily towards his mother but suddenly fell; the unexpected impact of the tarmac below was a shock he did not anticipate or enjoy and he screamed with all the force he could muster. The mother rushed to his aid, took him in her arms and comforted him with a genuine warmth that Myra could only strive after. She looked down at her own child and sighed. Miriam was confused for a moment to hear the distress of a fellow human being but she soon focused on the other children and their cries of delight.

As they walked on, the slight breeze blew a few leaves down from the trees and they danced in circles, swirling around in front of the buggy. It was as if an excitement buzzer had been pressed in Miriam's tummy button; she suddenly spread out her arms and legs like a human star, then she giggled loudly. She was totally fascinated by all around her. Two magpies screeched at them from the safety of the branches above, scolding them for encroaching on their private domain: trespassers would not be tolerated quietly. A group of pigeons held court on the central grassy area, bobbing their heads in mutual agreement with surprisingly mellifluous deep-throated cooing. One decided to abandon the meeting and took off; fluttering its wings and flying

e

above their heads with an aerial swoosh. Much higher in the sky the seagulls laughed at the antics of those beneath them in the full knowledge that they held ultimate control over all below.

Not only were there birds, but a handful of squirrels dotted around the park bounded with giant leaps from the base of one tree to the next, occasionally stopping to scan the surroundings, scratch at the ground under their feet or clamber up a tree to practise their arboreal acrobatics.

The pond also proved to be a fascinating section of the park. Miriam desperately tried to lean forward as far as she could and screwed up her eyes to see the goldfish swimming below the surface of the water. Myra wondered at their abundance as standing stock still in the centre of the pond was a small heron, an ominous statue, ready to dart forward and end the carefree life of any unsuspecting fish foolhardy enough to swim within its range.

On their way back from the park, two joggers pounded past them, breathing heavily. Myra was not a road runner but she used to keep herself reasonably fit in the local gymnasium. She would do a stint on the rowing machine and then on the cross-trainer. She would dabble with some weight lifting, but only up to about eight to ten kilograms. The guy at the reception desk took a shine to her and would let her in free; she smiled to herself at the thought. The arrival of Miriam had put a stop to all of that.

When they returned to the apartment, Miriam was so tired that she fell into a contented sleep. Myra left her in the buggy, walked past a dying pot plant, grabbed herself a drink which the pot plant would have benefited from, and made her way to her study.

What Myra did not think about on the way home or when they arrived was the fact that from the moment she and Miriam left the apartment to the moment they returned, not once did she speak to her daughter. More importantly, for her at least, the next part of the manuscript was lodged firmly in her head and, after a few brief notes, she was ready to start typing again.

Myra's manuscript notes:

Beauty of outside world
Sanctuary
Sleep at last?

Fiction

The Manuscript
Part Six

Outside The Wall

"It's all so. . . so. . . green and fresh." Tania looked in sheer delight at all around her. "Oh!" She jumped back as a small grey creature bounded across the ground in front of her; it stopped at the base of a large tree. It tickled its nose with its small forearms and then seemed to scrabble at the ground as if digging for treasure. "What is that? Oh, hang on, I think that I might have seen a picture; it's a squirrel and look at its wonderful tail."

Silva could not help but smile. "Yes, it's a squirrel. It has probably hidden an acorn in the ground at the base of the tree."

"There used to be red ones and grey ones, I think. But the red ones died out in the late twenty-first century."

"I'm impressed. You are well informed."

Tania felt her face redden but was soon distracted by other overwhelming features of her surroundings: the flora, the fauna, the scents, the sounds. An amazingly infectious smile lit up her whole face and her body was taut with excitement. Then she whispered for fear that the spoken voice might break the spell, "Listen. Listen. Can you hear it?"

"Birdsong."

"But there are not just the songs of birds, the trees are whispering too, telling so many secrets. You must listen."

The man looked down upon this child; her face shone with wonder. For a moment the worries, the struggles and the fear dissipated. He had been drowning in a sea of pressure and this effervescent young girl possessed the capability of providing a glimmer of hope to so many people for the future. But how? She alone could not rid society of all that was wrong. Yet, for the moment, she was not alone; he was with her. Her next request was unexpected.

"This is where I want to scatter my mother's ashes. She would have loved it here." She looked up to the man by her side. "Can I?"

"Yes, of course you can." He was taken aback but could certainly make those arrangements at some point. This moment, however, had to be shattered. He could not falter now. "We must go."

He quickly walked over to a seemingly overgrown area of brambles, creepers and branches which he started to pull back. Hidden beneath this jungle of foliage and greenery were a number of strange looking vehicles, smaller than any car Tania had ever seen but comprising three wheels, a seat and horizontal bars. Yet the body of the vehicle seemed to be missing. Silva pushed two of the vehicles into the clearing and threw odd branches and creepers back to hide the others that were there.

He showed Tania how to sit on the saddle area and how to start the purring sound that gave life to the machine. He showed her how to steer with the handles to go left or right. These vehicles did not possess the voice recognition or the internal programming that powered the vehicles within the walled confines of the city. The rider was the one with the control: no computer; no android. All the movement was the responsibility of one human being; nothing else. Even Silva was moved by this feeling of total control.

He assured Tania that there was a fairly clear pathway that they could follow and even if they veered off, the auto-bike could cope with any difficult terrain. Tania was not afraid. She put downward pressure on the starting button and smiled; the comforting purr beneath her felt empowering. She put her foot on the paddle that Silva had referred to as an accelerator and with a jolt she juddered forward.

"It will take a while, but you'll soon get used to it and even if you fall, the ground is not far away!" At last he felt that a light touch of humour would not be misplaced.

Tania followed in the path of Silva. She loved the feel of the natural breeze flowing through her hair; it was so refreshing after the claustrophobic, artificial atmosphere of Lithport. She was free. She had never felt like this before, except perhaps in her dreams, but this was real. This was the way life should be; not the regime in which she and all the other grey people existed.

All too soon, Silva slowed down his auto-bike and Tania followed. They came to a small clearing. Silva alighted from the bike, moved over to another tangle of branches and foliage and, as before, pulled away the greenery, which Tania now noticed was cleverly attached to and woven into a huge piece of cloth. She also pushed her bike there and Silva threw the heavy cloth of foliage over both of the vehicles with such ease that it might just as well have been a thin cotton sheet being thrown over a bed.

"I can't stay long. People will wonder where I am." He turned and walked through some of the trees, over protruding roots, under low hanging branches until they came to their destination. Tania could just decipher a whirring sound from above, she was unsure what it was but Silva seemed unperturbed as he knelt down, removed another large cloth, this time covered in a smoother, shorter spread of green. "Moss," he said without turning to her. Each utterance he now gave seemed more clipped than before; his whole demeanour had become more businesslike, but still she could not probe his mind.

A tunnel was revealed, large enough for the two of them to walk down side by side but Tania held back slightly, tentatively following in his wake. Within about fifty metres, they came to a door. Silva put the flat palm of his hand to the right of the door which slid open and they entered an underground apartment. The door then slid back behind them with a quiet whisper which caused Tania to turn momentarily and look back as the tunnel connecting them to the outside world disappeared from view.

An elegant young female walked smilingly towards them. Her khaki and brown boyish clothes could not hide the beautifully slim figure. This girl, if indeed she could still be described as a girl for she must have been about eighteen or nineteen, would probably have looked just as stunning dressed in a black plastic bag. Her large dark eyes were set deep within her smooth skin, untouched by the ravages of time. Her complexion was soft and slightly tanned, surprisingly so considering much of her life must be spent below ground or, if out, under a dense canopy of trees. Tania wanted to reach forward and just touch the thick flowing *brown hair. She felt a sense of familiarity with this young woman, a nugget of recognition, but said nothing and blocked any such thoughts from her mind. The young woman herself seemed more interested in Silva, on whom she focused her attention, rather than on Tania.*

"Let me introduce you to Mary. She will look after you. I must go." And with that brief introduction, Silva abruptly turned and went back from whence the two of them had come.

Tania immediately sensed a momentary wave of disappointment, almost dejection, in Mary's mind. There was something more between the two of them. Mary looked briefly towards the departing Silva and then returned her beautiful smiling gaze to Tania. "Welcome. You must be hungry and thirsty. Let me show you to the kitchen. Most of the girls are out getting food, but Kim is in the kitchen so I can introduce you to her. We have all been looking forward to meeting you. I am sorry about the death of your mother."

It seemed that they knew about her circumstances and had been expecting her arrival. "Don't be concerned, we get regular updates from inside The Wall."

As Tania and Mary walked towards what the latter called the kitchen, each step seemed to ignite a light in front of them. No one would ever have realised that they were underground; there were even windows on both sides with small, neatly kept gardens beyond.

As they approached the kitchen, succulent scents wafted towards them both. There was a clattering of pans and from out of the steamy atmosphere emerged a much shorter girl, probably of a similar age to Mary, but that was where the similarity ended. She too wore khaki and brown but her clothes were ill-fitting and made her look even more dumpy and boyish. She wiped the sweat from her brow and bounded forward, her large breasts bouncing up and down. She smiled, just as Mary had done, but this smile was genuine; this smile did not mask inner turmoil. "Hi. Welcome. I've been really looking forward to meeting you. I'm Kimberley but everyone calls me Kim."

She held out her arm and Tania expected her to shake hands, but Kim took Tania's arm, pulled her forwards and gave her a huge all-embracing hug, totally smothering the tiny frame of the new arrival in the ample khaki bosoms.

"There's some water boiling in the pan; I'm afraid we don't

possess an automatic boiling water button here; we have to boil our own. A lot of the stuff we have is pretty much up-to-date but not everything. We don't have any Service Mechanics here, as I am sure you realise."

"Mind you," interjected Mary, "Kim is a dab hand at fixing and mending."

Kim ignored the compliment, but coloured as if the compliment meant a lot to her, and then carried on regardless. "Fruit tea, with fruit from our very own garden? Or something colder?"

"Fruit tea, please," Tania replied.

"Apple or lemon? Actually I might have some mint left, if you'd prefer."

"Apple would be lovely, thank you."

"And what about something to eat? You look as though you could do with something to eat. In fact, you look as though you haven't had a good meal in ages. Dinner won't be for about another hour when everyone returns, so perhaps you would like a quick snack. I've got some hummus here and you can dip in some crunchy veg or some breadsticks. Or how about a handful of homemade biscuits?"

Tania simply adored this bubbly girl who just seemed to say what she thought, but she certainly didn't get the same impression of Mary. She thought that Mary's mind was reaching out slightly negatively towards Kim, rejecting the effusiveness and openness. "Homemade biscuits sound great."

Kim reached across to a large odd shaped pot. "It's a teddy bear. I'm not too sure what a teddy bear is, but it says teddy bear on the base. I think it's rather sweet, but I've never seen a live teddy bear anywhere here or anywhere else come to that, so I don't know if it's an animal from the past that became extinct like so many others or something just made up. I did some research and found lots of information on different types of bear: grizzly bears, panda bears, polar bears, brown bears, black bears and even blue bears, just like this biscuit pot, but no teddy bears. I once knew a girl called Teddy, but she wasn't blue.

"We do get creatures here. You'd be amazed: creatures that walk; creatures that fly; even creatures that slither and," at which point her face folded into a screwed up paper ball of disgust, "eat my vegetables and leave gooey mucus everywhere! Nasty, slimy things! Some even curl up into little shells to

*protect themselves. Although I must admit that some of the shells
are really pretty."*

*All of this was said with such alacrity and speed; Kim seemed
to be able to talk without pausing for breath. "Sorry, I talk too
much."*

*Tania smiled and took a bite from one of the biscuits that Kim
offered her. One day she would tell her the stories of A. A. Milne's
'Winnie the Pooh' but for the moment she was overwhelmed by
the sensational taste of the biscuits, not like anything she had ever
eaten before. She suddenly realised just how hungry she was.*

*"I use the cinnamon and ginger we grow here in our own
gardens. Cinnamon's easy to grow, as long as the soil is kept
slightly dry, a potted cinnamon plant can thrive for years without
special care. And ginger, well that's a tropical plant but it can
still be grown quite easily and doesn't require much expert
knowledge. The seed tray needs to be kept indoors though,
because most ginger is not winter hardy."*

*Kim might not know a lot about teddy bears, but she certainly
knew about plants. However, Tania was far more interested in the
biscuits themselves rather than their ingredients.*

*Kim started to laugh at the way Tania just took bite after bite
after bite. "It's nice to know that my baking is appreciated. When
you've had your fill, I will show you around the place. The dinner
doesn't need any attention now; it can just bubble away merrily
until the girls return."*

*She paused briefly and looked disappointed that Mary had
gone. Tania could feel Mary's presence in the apartment, but it
was distant, yet the strength of emotions within her mindset were
there for Tania to read: confusion and pain.*

*"Mary's beautiful." What an inane comment to make, but she
just wanted to find out a little more about the reason for the
undoubted reticence. Kim smiled; she could sense Tania's
curiosity, but she was not about to fully divulge all her secrets.*

"Mary gets a little upset from time to time."

*Perhaps this was a gentle warning that it was too early to be
overly inquisitive; they did not know each other well enough yet.
But Kim was so bubbly, so open, and so honest that Tania knew it
would not be long before she told Tania all she wanted to know.*

*"When you arrived, I expect you saw the gardens on either
side of the entrance tunnel. A number of trees were removed from*

there and it gets a lot of light so the vegetables and herbs flourish. There are some more gardens behind this building but they hold the more hardy plants that don't need so much attention, like potatoes, but there's loads of colour because we have planted lots of edible flowers for salads, cakes, sauces and. . ."

"Biscuits," laughed Tania.

"Yes, and biscuits. Come and have a look."

They left the kitchen and immediately walked into an open area but hidden from the outside world by overhanging trees. They were not alone as another girl was walking along a row of plants picking some of the flowers and placing them into a basket which had become an ensemble of colour. These gardens were clearly lovingly tended. Kim called over to the young girl, "Suky, meet Tania. She's just arrived."

Suky smiled, shouted hi and continued to fill her basket with pansies, sweet violets, nasturtium and mixed marigolds. She happily hummed a tune as she walked up and down the rows of flowers.

"Suky loves being here. She spends hours in the gardens."

After spending time strolling around the grounds, meeting more girls and being really impressed by the industriousness of this completely alien yet natural environment, Tania returned inside with Kim.

Kim then showed her the gymnasium and laughingly said that she could not remember the last time she had been there; there were no compulsory armbands for people here recording the number of steps taken during the week, and no visiting Service Officials to take anyone on a 'Health Recover Course' if the required number had not been achieved. Tania met three other girls there, doing some exercises on various machines and weight lifting. She did not think that she could even lift the weights from the ground, let alone raise them above her head as these girls were doing.

Despite the evident pleasure Tania exhibited for all that Kim showed her on the guided tour, the young new arrival was clearly very tired. Kim took her to her sleeping capsule, already engraved with her name above, and she soon fell asleep without the need of any Inducing Slumber Lozenge. It was a deep, dreamless sleep; after all that happened over the past few hours, she was sure that she could be happy here.

Scattering the ashes

Silva was true to his word, and a few days later he returned to the community safe house with the urn that held Nina Alexander's ashes. However, his visit occurred during the evening when all of the residents were fully engaged in enjoying the food and the community spirit that was generated by spending their suppertime together. He was unseen by all and his presence was detected by only one vigilant female resident who was considered by many to have a gift.

The timing and the fact that he left the urn by the front entrance of the building was perceived by more than one person in the community as being deliberate. A handwritten note was attached to the urn, its message being that he had fulfilled his promise to the young new arrival and hoped she was now able to say her final goodbye to her mother.

He did not stay. On hearing of his fleeting visit, Mary disappeared for a number of hours.

Tania had not wanted a fuss. She just wanted to take the urn into the wood, say a few words, scatter the ashes and then start her new life, just as her mother would have wished. None of the girls had known her mother. She felt that this was something she had to do alone and in private. Kim, however, had other ideas and was not going to let that happen; the rest of the safe house community may not have known her mother but they had all experienced loss. They would all be there and, inevitably, Kim would lay on a veritable feast for them afterwards.

At first Tania protested, but her protestations, which to be perfectly honest lacked real conviction, simply fell on deaf ears. In the end she was persuaded that Kim was right. Tania needed to accept that she was part of a close community and although she had not been there very long, she had to realise that from now on nothing of any significance should be carried out in isolation. Scattering her mother's ashes was certainly a significant moment. The other girls would always be there for her and she would always be there for them: a mutually beneficial arrangement. It would take a long time for her to adapt to this way of life, but she would try.

Every girl in that community had a right to participate in the

106

grieving process, albeit their own personal grieving process, and in the ultimate celebration of a mother's life.

They congregated outside in a large open area; the weather was dry with a slight refreshing breeze in the air. Before the ashes were scattered, the urn was passed from one community member to the next. Each girl was given the opportunity to hold the receptacle and its contents for a few moments. Some took this opportunity and openly affirmed their prepared farewells whilst others whispered quiet words of solace and comfort: their own personal epitaph for lost family members. A handful of girls passed the receptacle on, not feeling the need for further closure.

Finally the urn reached Tania. She cradled it in her arms. Her mother was there with her; she felt her presence and knew that she always would. Her throat was tight; her eyes misted over, but she looked up to the skies above and spoke for all to hear, "I love you." Her words hung in the air for a few moments before being taken by the breeze.

The lid was removed and the ashes were scattered. Nina Alexander, who had exuded so much influence on Tania's life, could not be reduced to just a handful of dust; she was more than that and her loving spirit wholly possessed this moment. And, as if in mutual understanding, the birds in the trees sang and chirruped their own compassion. Tania watched as the last specks of ash, like grey snowflakes, fell to the ground and became the earth.

A few moments later, having given her time for contemplation, Kim touched her lightly on the shoulder, "Your mother would have been proud of you."

Tania could only nod in response. Words were unnecessary.

There was a silence. Although it seemed that no one now knew what to say, it was not an awkward silence but a silence in which every single girl held her own thoughts close to her heart.

"Time for food." Kim was inevitably the one to break that silence, instinctively waiting briefly for when the time was right.

They all walked back to the house in loose clusters.

Kim walked beside Tania. "How do you feel?"

Tania was honest in her response, "I'm alright. It's hard and it always will be, but I'll be alright."

"I know." Kim smiled and Tania smiled back.

Reality

Chapter Seven

Howie Redman

The distinctive ting of the lift and the luminescent number on the visual display above the doors combined to indicate that Myra and Miriam had arrived at the floor of their apartment after their second walk to the park within a matter of days. Myra pushed the buggy out into the corridor to discover that her front door was blocked by a ladder. Dressed in his old blue overalls, Howie Redman, the council maintenance engineer, was on the fourth rung reaching across to the fire alarm above her threshold.

Howie had heard the lift arrive and seemed a little perplexed at Myra's arrival. "Oh, sorry miss, I won't be a minute. I'm fixing the cover back on this fire alarm; it seems to have become a bit loose. I'm just doing my regular rounds and checking that everything is spick and span. Everything on this floor seems to be in full working order."

Myra grinned. She had always been taken by his strong Liverpudlian accent. "And I thought that was a camera up there."

Howie's face flushed, "Oh no, nothing like that."

The distinctive sound of a furtively opened door further down the corridor was not lost on either of them. Howie easily recognised the familiar mischievous twinkle in Myra's eyes and waited for the inevitable biting comment. Without turning, she spoke as if in conversation with him yet raised her voice, "It would be pretty interesting to have a camera up there. All the comings and goings. All the skulking strangers from the underworld creeping about. All the illicit visitors I get every hour of every day and night." Then, just to make her point, she added more loudly but still without turning, "Isn't that so Mr Mortnel?"

This was swiftly followed by the click of a closing door.

Howie Redman made his way slowly and carefully down the slightly wobbly ladder and moved it to one side. "You are a one, miss." He took a step back, bowed and swept his arm towards Myra's front door. "Well, it's all yours, ma'm."

The young lady's triumphal air of a small victory won made him smile. He watched her disappear into her apartment with a spring in her step that he had not seen for a long time. He folded up the ladder and continued up to the next floor. Safety maintenance was his priority, but he had to admit that the building's residents were certainly an interesting bunch, especially on this particular level.

When Myra went into her study, leaving her daughter asleep in her buggy, she sauntered over to her computer desk and jotted down just five simple words on her notepad. Five words that were not of her own creativity, but five words that to all intents and purposes seemed to sum up where she would go from here with her manuscript.

Myra's manuscript notes:

BIG BROTHER IS WATCHING YOU

Fiction

The Manuscript
Part Seven

Rusty

Russell Howard sat looking at the array of CCTV images in front of him. Even when sitting down he was restless, ever on the alert for any change of routine, anything unexpected. There were many screens, covering both outside the building and inside the building. He knew the location of every single person who ventured onto the screen and recognised each of them individually, not just their physical appearance but also as individual beings with individual personalities and characteristics.

Outside, for example, there was Tom carrying out his security responsibilities in a slightly less than secure way. A smile and a few polite words seemed to give anyone access to the place. Tom was too trusting.

Inside, Russell could accurately predict who would be walking down what corridor and when; who would be entering which cupboard and what would be removed or replaced; and who would be in which office. Even without seeing their faces he could recognise each person's way of moving: George's rather lop-sided waddle with his left leg slightly shorter than his right; and Helen's purposeful glide with her long blonde hair pulled back into a single, plaited ponytail and secured with a red band - always red, never any other colour: her own touch of defiance against the dull uniform. There was Kilman with his forthright stride, walking down the centre of the corridor as if an alarm would suddenly kick into action should he happen to veer to the left or right and inadvertently touch either wall. He expected everyone to move out of his way; his own course was unwavering. Silva, in contrast, had a loping, almost languid stride. Then there was Lisa with her small feet and petite frame trotting down the corridor in her heels of silver: her own small personal demonstration against the dull laboratory coat all technicians had to wear. He always smiled when he watched her. They all knew the cameras were there, but they had accepted them and blanked them from their everyday movements.

He was not content with merely sitting in an office, looking at cameras. There was usually another member of the team there who could do that, although not so expertly as he did. Russell would walk the corridors, not following any routine that anyone could calculate, but ensuring that he was thorough. Sometimes he would slightly alter his route, sometimes he would just slightly alter the timings: a minute earlier here; a minute later there.

Having felt that he had sat down for long enough and needing to stretch his legs, he made his way out into the corridors of power. He turned the corner just in time to see Kilman unlocking and entering Silva's office, yet he knew that Silva was not there. In fact, he had been asked to keep a close eye on that area today.

Russell decided to let diplomacy be the order of the day and suddenly developed a tickly cough while inspecting the state of the fire alarm further down the corridor. Within seconds, almost instantaneously in fact, Kilman entered the corridor from Silva's office. "Mr Howard." Kilman was the only member of staff who never referred to the chief watchman as Rusty. "On your rounds," which he proffered as a rather obvious statement and not a question.

"Yes, sir."

"Good." Kilman paused. "Mr Silva left his door slightly open so I just wanted to check that everything was okay, but it all seems to be in order. As you're here, will you lock up, please? My keys are in my office."

Russell knew that Kilman's keys were not in his office; only moments before that he had seen him use them to unlock the senior officer's door. Surely he had not forgotten the cameras? What would he have said if confronted with this oversight? But

111

Russell was a professional; he kept his mouth closed. For the moment.

"Yes, of course, sir."

With that, Kilman returned to his own office nearby.

When Russell returned to the screen room, young Ben had been surveying the scene, "Saw you talking to Kilman in the corridor. Screen was fuzzy before that. Don't know what was wrong with it. Tapped it, but that didn't seem to do any good. Been happening quite a lot recently. Don't know why. Perhaps we should get maintenance in."

Not for the first time, Rusty wondered how Ben had ever got this far in his career, not that Ben needed to talk in fully grammatical sentences but sometimes his clipped style of speech left vital details hovering in the air without any useful explanation. And there was never any sense of urgency. He should have informed Russell before if this fuzziness had been 'happening quite a lot recently'. Russell, however, was fully aware of the issue and knew exactly what the problem was and its origin. In fact, he could whittle it down to two men who occasionally wished to conceal their actions: he had just spoken with one of them in the corridor a few moments before whilst standing outside the other one's office.

Rusty had already had the maintenance complete a full service and maintenance check but with little success. Nothing wrong had been found with the system and he had the distinct impression that he was being patronised as a rather over-fussy old warrior. So he did a little investigative work himself in a couple of select offices.

Silva's return caught his eye.

Another Confrontation

Vary rarely did Silva stretch his limbs to their full extent to stride so resolutely down the corridor, but the occasion necessitated it today. He had spent an hour or two with Lisa after his return from the world outside The Wall; she, of course, was blissfully unaware of where he had been. He knew that he needed to end the affair soon; it had petered out and lost its purpose. Lisa had been a fairly useful source of information, but not as useful as he had originally hoped. He had even risked being seen in public with her on a few occasions. The risk of gossip outweighed the possibility of gaining her confidence. Not long ago he had taken her to an evening concert in anticipation of procuring inside information on any women's movements. The evening had been a disappointment both in terms of the cacophonous noise, purported to be music, to which they were exposed and the lack of any useful intelligence from her. Indeed, he had a niggling feeling that she knew more than she was prepared to confide. Was he taking advantage of her or was she taking advantage of him?

He knew exactly where he was going. He did not turn into his own office but marched purposefully into Kilman's. The closed door was no barrier to him; it was swiftly opened and closed behind him in one sweeping move.

"I would like you to explain your actions the other evening, Kilman. I do not recall giving instructions for you to inspect my laboratories and frighten my staff."

Kilman appeared unperturbed. "There were some anomalies in the test results from our staff. A pattern had started to emerge and I felt that you had more serious concerns than this. I didn't want to worry you over something that could have turned out, as it did, to be of little significance."

"You're an idiot, Kilman! Go home. Make love to your wife or your mistress should you so wish, although you're so damned righteous, you wouldn't even contemplate another woman would you? Forget all of this. You nearly ruined everything with your bloody interference." He turned and left.

Kilman mulled over the parting words: "Wouldn't even contemplate another woman." Silva was right as far as actually loving another woman was concerned, but that was not of any significance at the moment, what was important was that he had certainly provoked Silva and that was what he had wanted to do. The man would make a major mistake soon; he was sure of that.

Reality

Chapter Eight

A Good Idea

Anita Mann had just managed to reverse park her Fiat car into the smallest of spaces outside her house when the distinctive ring of her mobile played its ridiculous tune. She really needed to change that tune; it would take a matter of seconds but she had just not got around to doing it. Taking the phone from her pocket, she checked the number and recognised it immediately, "Hi Myra."

"Hi. How are you progressing with the reading of my new manuscript? I think it's about time you came around again to give me your expert opinion. I know it's not finished but I'm sure you've had some reaction to it and I enjoy listening to your ideas on what I've written."

"Oh great. Yes, I've finished reading what you've done so far. I enjoyed it. It made a welcome change from The Baird; I'm a bit fed up with him at the moment."

"Well I don't think it's quite up to the stratospheric level of Shakespeare but I'm glad you've enjoyed what you've read so far. How about coming round one weekend? Saturday week? I'll pass the next bit of my epic to you. How ever much I've done by then. I've got a few ideas."

"Yes, that'll be great."

"You sound weary. Bad day at the office?"

"Not really. I had to break up a fight in the playground. One boy, a notorious thug to be honest, although I am sure his doting parents think he's a little darling. Well, he absolutely knocked the living daylights out of another. Mind you, I shouldn't think that the recipient of the thrashing was entirely innocent either. He's a bit of a weasel.

"God knows where the member of staff who was supposed to be on duty was hanging out; he'll be for the high jump, unless of course it was a senior team leader who'll no doubt have some excuse. Anyway, I managed to calm the lads down, before a couple of other staff members arrived and I called the ambulance. Then, of course, I had to fill in all the details in the Incident Log Book. I've only just got home. I need a strong dose of caffeine."

"Sounds awful. But you're always calm in a crisis, Anita. I'll see you Saturday week and we'll have a glass or two, or even three, of wine. Come round about seven to half past. Okay?"

"Yep, see you then. Bye for now." Anita looked forward to that. She had not seen her friend for a few weeks and it would be good to catch up. She might also get a chance to see Miriam, as she really doted on that little girl. Not only that, she always looked forward to reading Myra's early manuscripts and wondered what direction this one was going to take next.

The brief chat had rekindled Myra's ideas regarding the development of the plot, "A physical confrontation. Of course, why on earth didn't I think of that before? That will get rid of Kilman for a while."

Myra's manuscript notes:

Violence
Fortunate intervention

Fiction

The Manuscript
Part Eight

May Kilman

"Where the bloody hell is my folder?" A red eyed and a red faced Kilman was screaming uncontrollably now as he strode towards his wife. *"I need my folder. Today is the day. This is my day. He's not going to ruin it for me. I am going to expose him and all he stands for and then look out. He thinks he can swan off without telling anyone where he's going. I've written down all the times he's left the office and how long he has been out. He should be as accountable as the next man; I don't care if he's the boss."* Not one breath was taken during this long vehement harangue.

Her husband's eyes bore into her very soul. May knew where the folder was; in fact, it was not that difficult to find. The precious folder lay under Kilman's bed where he had put it; where he always put it; where she had replaced it, having scrutinised every page from top to bottom. She had carefully wiped over the cover and then allowed herself that brief feeling of excitement that comes with doing something slightly risqué: a mischievous self-indulgent tinge of rebelliousness as she saw the bedding naturally fell on to it. She had not fully understood everything that she had read; much of it comprised the use of technical jargon with which she was unfamiliar. However, she was afforded some insight that gave her an idea of what was going on. She had put it back exactly where it had originally been placed so that she could not be accused of moving it; her

116

husband had just not looked carefully in his haste to find it. If she had actually hidden it in some dark corner of the apartment, she would have had no defence regarding its whereabouts; not that it mattered as he would never listen to any justification, especially from her.

She was very tempted to tell him exactly where it was, or where she thought it might be, but she gained some meagre sense of satisfaction that she knew something he didn't know. Perhaps her sense of satisfaction was reflected in her face as, within seconds he was upon her. His right arm struck her head with such force that she reeled backwards. Her whole body twisted. She reached out with both arms towards the kitchen sideboard to save herself from falling to the ground. And there it was: a lethal weapon just lying there innocently.

Without another thought, she grabbed the handle. She gripped the black plastic surface and turned. She plunged the knife forward. Everything happened so quickly.

Kilman stopped. He stared in disbelief. He grimaced: a terrifying grimace. His body becoming less tense, his whole being deflated and he whispered, "I'm sorry. I'm so sorry." And then he fell.

May stood there and looked down at the monster who was now no more. She dropped the knife and it fell with an echoing clatter to the floor. Her domestic ordeal was over.

It was over for her and unbeknown to her, it was over for the many innocent people her husband could have saved. She had unwittingly destroyed the one person who could have saved the Elevationists.

May was frozen to the spot, unable to speak, but within the seconds that to her seemed interminable, there was a banging at the door. Lisa Watts had been walking past. She heard the shouting from outside. She knew who owned the apartment: Silva had spat out his deputy's name every time they surreptitiously drove by in his company limousine. She screamed at the doorway and banged it with her fists. Finally, May came to her senses, walked calmly to the door as if in a trance, opened it and looked at this woman. "I've killed him."

Lisa pushed past her and entered the apartment, rushing purposefully across the room to the kitchen.

"I'll get this cleared up. You need to come with me now. I know *where you can go. It'll be safe. You'll be okay."*

Lisa calmly but firmly directed May to the door, grabbing an outdoor jacket on the way and wrapping it around the stunned woman's shoulders. She knew exactly what to do and who to get to clear up the mess.

Reality

Chapter Nine

April 2018

Anita sat on the soft, expansive corner sofa and stretched out her legs along the cushions. She looked around the room. She thought, not ungraciously or with any envy, how well Myra had done for herself: the whole situation seemed surreal and to the outside observer rather unfair. There she was, Miss Anita Mann BAHons, MEd, a fully qualified teacher of English, living in a small bedsit, paying an extortionate rent to a covetous landlord. Myra, on the other hand, had left school at sixteen; worked briefly in a corner shop; then briefly as a waitress; then briefly as an usher in the local cinema. She took a couple of writing courses and began her authorial career with some success, but nothing exceptional. However, it was the first occupation with which she seemed to have felt some sense of bonding and, as such, had persevered with it. During these various 'careers' she had met a number of totally unsuitable blokes, got herself pregnant and here she was, Miss Myra Vilas, in a luxurious, modern three bedroomed apartment: a present from her wealthy but absent father.

The room in which Anita sat was painted cream but had exotic metallic and very modern hangings on each wall. To her left was an elegant long legged crane: tall and grey bodied with a distinctive crimson-capped head. Behind her and between the two large windows overlooking the distant park, was an owl, possibly a horned owl or an eagle owl, with each feather individually fashioned to reflect the light of the fire opposite. To her right was her favourite: the metal wall art sea turtle. There were no gaudy colours, just a beautiful silver-coloured steel sea turtle swimming seemingly effortlessly over some seaweed. And in front of her above the fire was the iridescent Alkeme metal tree of life symbolising wisdom and protection.

Myra, the beautiful long limbed, slim and elegant Myra, certainly seemed protected from the hardships that life often threw at mere mortals, especially those who had decided to enter the realms of pedagogy and take on the responsibility of the lowly school teacher. Teaching was an occupation viewed by a sanguine few as a worthy vocation, educating our future generation. However, it was viewed by the young recipients of that education as a job for buffoons and fools who were there to be ridiculed mercilessly or used as a sounding board for the blossoming future generation's bravado, like the 'lovely' Wayne who had, only that day, told Miss Anita Mann to "F--- off back to where she came from." She did not deign to ask him where he thought she came from.

On the mantelpiece was a colourful ornament which she recognised as one she had given to Myra for her birthday two years previously. It looked a little less vivid than she remembered but still took pride of place. The seahorse had attracted her attention in the shop window of the town's wonderful art and craft shop. The moment she saw it she had thought of the appeal such a creature would have for Myra. A creature where the female deposited the eggs into the male's pouch during mating and where they stayed until the male gave birth to the young. She had not believed for one moment that her friend would ever contemplate becoming pregnant herself; but if the male became pregnant and had to carry the young, that might have been a different story! How wrong she had been.

She got up and walked over to the mantelpiece where she lifted up the seahorse. She was surprised to see a ring of dust around where the ornament had stood, and then realised on closer scrutiny that everywhere about her a fine dust had settled. She heard Myra returning and quickly replaced the object but not quickly enough to go unnoticed.

Myra held two large and very welcome glasses of white wine. "Here, this will take your mind off the dust!"

"I wasn't looking at the dust. I was just looking at the seahorse and thinking about when I got it from the shop and had the audacity to offer a lower price. The shopkeeper was really miffed."

Myra totally ignored her case for the defence. "Don't worry, Anita. I gave my cleaner notice to leave over a month ago and I just haven't got round to cleaning in here recently. It might have something to do with that other little creature in the next room. That little monkey of mine has finally gone to sleep and we can relax."

She carefully placed one of the glasses in front of her friend, and Anita immediately took a sip. "This is nice. What brand is it?"

"Oh, I didn't really take any notice of that. I just saw that it was Sauvignon Blanc, which I know you like, and it had a picture of a swan on the label, which I rather liked. So a win win scenario!"

Back on more comfortable ground, Anita changed the subject to one of Myra's neighbours. "That Corporal Dead Ringer, as you call him, was peeking out of his door when I arrived, the nosey old parker."

"Oh, he's not only nosey but I'm absolutely positive he's a dirty old man too! I am sure I saw him kerb crawling the other day. I mean, his huge Bentley is pretty distinctive, isn't it?"

"Perhaps he was just driving slowly; he is in his eighties, isn't he? Anyway, I keep meaning to ask you why you call him Corporal Dead Ringer. I am sure that's not his name."

Myra smiled. "No, he's only seventy-six and I'm amazed that he has reached that age to be honest with you; he is always blustering about and the arguments he has with his wife are just a nightmare to hear. He shouts and screams; he calls her all sorts of names. Sometimes I think that one of them is going to kill the other, and if not I often wonder if he might have a heart attack, he gets so worked up.

"As for his rank in the services, I don't think he was a corporal: far too lowly a rank for him. He had some long winded title, like Warrant Officer Class 1. Too much of a mouthful for me, so I call him Corporal. As for the Dead Ringer, his actual name is Mortnel. As you know, just like you, I enjoy playing with words, especially people's names. It's my little joke: 'mort' being, as I'm sure you are aware, Latin for dead and 'knell' the sound a bell makes at a funeral, or so I'm told. I've never heard a bell ring at a funeral;

f

not that I've been to many." Her eyes misted over as she tried desperately to blank her own mother's funeral from her mind.

Anita listened with interest, realised the change of tone in her friend's voice and deliberately turned her gaze towards the coffee table on which lay a large ream of stapled papers: duplicates of those which she had read at home.

Myra followed her gaze. "Well, what do you think?" she asked. The answer was succinct. "It's good."

"Nothing more to say? Just 'Good'? That's not like you!"

Anita took a deep breath. "I think it's well written and I enjoyed reading it."

"But. . ." Myra waited for the inevitable.

"The bad guy is a bit obvious. It has to be Kilman. Think about Agatha Christie detective novels. She makes sure that there are usually about five or more possible perpetrators of the crime and this always leaves the reader guessing to the very end. With your book, it's really easy to eliminate everyone except Kilman."

"So you think this is a detective novel and a crime has been committed? And the reader has to work out who has committed the crime?"

"Well you usually write crime stories, although not set in the future, and there's certainly a dead woman – Tania's mother – and I'm pretty sure that she's been murdered. She wouldn't kill herself would she? Mind you, I think the basis of the society is actually barbaric: getting people to believe that young girls are eliminated because they are intelligent and have an innate empathetic skill." Anita seemed to be on a roll.

"So how do you think the woman died?"

Anita was ready now and all her ideas poured forth like an unstoppable cascading waterfall. "She is clearly having an affair or has had an affair with Silva; the sections about the babies and the pregnancies are all a smoke-screen to this affair. I know you and the way your mind works. I didn't miss the throw away comment, 'The dark eyes that she had once looked into with affection. . .' Something is obviously going on between the two of them.

"All these years later, he regrets the way he treated her and her husband. He wants to make sure that Tania is safe. It's his way of achieving forgiveness. His catharsis, I suppose you might call it."

122

Myra smiled at the use of this word. One she had herself considered when first embarking on the writing of the manuscript.

Even for Anita, this topic was getting too close to reality, yet she was not going to be diverted. However, she did not want to mention Silva any further, knowing that he represented Arthur Vilas, Myra's father. A conversation about him would just turn into blaming and counter-blaming regarding the death of her mother. She turned her attention back to the villain of the piece. "Kilman is a bully. He's just a thug. He doesn't tolerate anyone standing in his way or anyone who might question or threaten the very fabric of the society of which he is a part. He finds out about the affair; he himself is in a loveless marriage and he is deeply jealous. When the date for the raid is arranged he arrives early as he really wants to get the girl – that's his job. He barges in to the house, knocks over Tania's mother who tries to stop him. She falls and, let's say for argument's sake, she knocks her head on the corner of a work surface and collapses with a wound that proves fatal. Silva rushes in, too late to save his mistress but is determined to find Tania before Kilman does.

"By the way, you could have done a really descriptive bit about how Tania's mother lies on the floor in a pool of blood. That would have been meaty."

Myra gave a brief sardonic laugh, "Meaty!"

"Well, you know what I mean. Readers like a bit of blood and gore."

"Perhaps your students like blood and gore as you so delicately put it, but they might not be my intended readership. And you don't know how Tania's mother died. Perhaps there wasn't any blood and gore."

"No, but it must have been Kilman. And by the way, his name is a bit pseudo-Shakespeare isn't it?"

"Pseudo-Shakespeare? What do you mean?"

"Well think of 'Twelfth Night', for example, and Sir Toby Belch, a drunkard who clearly did a lot of. . ."

"Belching?" suggested Myra as she reached for another sip of wine, realised that both glasses were empty and went to the kitchen area to retrieve the rest of the bottle and another one while she was there.

Anita continued in full flow. The effect of the alcohol certainly contributed towards the brevity of the previous conviction to avoid talking about Silva. "Yes. Then there's Silva, who is the knight in shining armour. The man who woos the ladies but has a heart of gold and has only ever truly loved one woman. He fights against the system and saves the day. Even the girl, Mary, falls madly in love with him. She can't get much opportunity to meet boys her own age. In fact, she doesn't have the opportunity to meet any men by the seem of it, so she fancies the pants off this rather grand older chap, whose name is clearly a play on the word 'silver'." She felt that this final assertion would avoid any comparisons with the real Mr Arthur Vilas.

"And talking of names: Mary is a bit old fashioned isn't it? This is supposed to be 2323. Names will have changed by then; I don't think biblical names will be at the top of the 'Most popular names to call your child in 2323' list!"

Myra ignored this and asked, "What about Kilman's headaches? How do you account for those? And, of course, you haven't had the chance to read the eighth part which I wrote as a result of our recent brief conversation."

"Our recent conversation?"

"The fight between two of your students."

"Oh yes, of course. So what happens in the eighth part?"

"It's very short. Here. Have a read." Myra passed the section over to Anita. "Basically, May Kilman stabs her husband with a kitchen knife."

This did not deter Anita. "His wife has been slowly poisoning him; that accounts for the headaches, but in the end she loses her patience. And, by the way, who can blame her? She kills him in a fit of temper.

"With Kilman dead, everyone can live happily ever after. Actually, Silva can go from strength to strength by highlighting the injustices of the society in which they live. The different sectors can be destroyed and the girls in exile can all return to the township from which they came."

She put her recently refilled glass down with such confidence and aplomb that a few drops splashed out onto the table and they both watched unmoving as the small damp dots seeped into the wood.

"Mind you, I'm not too sure about what you mean by this bit." She shuffled the paper into Myra's view and pointed at the section to which she was referring and read it out. "She had unwittingly destroyed the one person who could have saved the Elevationists."

Realising that she had perhaps got a little carried away, Anita took a deep breath and calmed herself before speaking again, more slowly this time. "Have you really visualised this 2323 society? Do you truly believe many of our means of communication, like the internet and mobiles, will be banned for all except those in pivotal governmental roles? And what about walls surrounding the different pockets of civilisation? That's a bit over the top, isn't it? Do you really think that will happen?"

"I don't know, Anita. It's certainly one interpretation, and after all, it is fiction and just one person's view of a possible future. Donald Trump talks about a wall between the United States and Mexico. Racism has become the scourge of our society and no one seems to have an answer; it might get to the point where large sections of the community will need to be divided.

"With regards to the internet, Wetherspoons are quitting social media saying that it's not vital for a successful business and that people spend too much time on Twitter, Instagram and Facebook and end up struggling to control their compulsion to do so. The terms of reference of Facebook and Instagram say that you shouldn't be on it if you are under the age of 13, but they don't do anything to police it. The guidelines for WhatsApp say you shouldn't be on it unless you're 16, but again they don't do anything to police it. Concern is also growing in our own government and medical circles about the effect of recreational screen use on children's ability to learn and acquire knowledge. Did you know that a study of people aged 18 to 24 in the United States last year found that 41 per cent of social media users thought that it made them feel sad, anxious or depressed? A report last year by the Education Policy Institute found a link between social media use and mental health. Look at all the cyber bullying that goes on; there has to be a way to put an end to it and that way might have to be quite drastic. Governments and even nations of the future might agree and start acting on these ideas. Who knows?"

Anita knew that the alcohol in her head would not allow her to counteract any argument along these lines and Myra had clearly done her research, even if some of her views seemed a bit skewed to her own way of thinking. Perhaps this discussion could be had another day. "You have certainly done your homework, Myra! The manuscript is really good and I can't wait to read the rest, but I do think it's about time I went home. It's been lovely seeing you again. I'll just ring for a taxi." She stood up to leave.

Not for the first time during the course of the evening, Myra seemed oblivious to what Anita said. In truth, she felt that she had to add what to her was a highly personal and poignant comment that Anita might have missed as being the essence of her writing. "It's really about the people in the manuscript. It's the people that matter."

Then she realised that Anita had stood up. "I'll send the rest of the manuscript to you in a week or two. I've got quite a lot of it down in draft form, I know what's going to happen, but it just needs a bit of tidying up."

"You've got it all sorted already?"

"Yes," Myra smiled wickedly, "but of course you have worked out exactly what happens. You've solved the puzzle."

"Oh, I might have got it all wrong."

Myra smiled again but this time with less joy; it was the enigmatic smile of a woman who knew all the answers to a conundrum but gained no pleasure from her knowledge.

She watched Anita go, closed the door behind her and then went to the window to see her closest of friends board the taxi which drove into the distant night. "Yes, you have got it all wrong."

Myra's Neighbours

It was early in the morning and after continuous ringing of her apartment bell and constant banging at the door itself, Myra eventually opened the portal to face the man standing at the threshold. She was not at all surprised by the identity of the noisy and unwelcome caller, "Yes, Mr Mortnel, what can I do for you? As I am sure you can hear, I have my hands full at the moment."

"Warrant Officer Mortnel to you, not Mr and yes I certainly can hear and that is what I am doing here; to get you to stop that infernal racket. If there's something wrong with your child get a doctor to her. Night and day I have to put up with all the crying; it's sending me mad."

It obviously was not sending his wife mad because he just

referred to himself and not to the two of them. Myra looked him straight in the eye, "Of course, you have never had any children yourself have you?"

"That's of no concern to you. Or has any relevance to the present situation."

Myra took a deep breath. "For a long time, Mr Mortnel, I have put up with your constant bickering and arguing with your wife. I have never complained. In fact, I have never even mentioned it. As time has gone on, I am glad to say that you must have sorted out your differences, to some degree at least, and I am truly grateful. I have been able to live in greater peace and quiet. To be honest, I have been very patient and now it is your turn to reciprocate."

"How dare you speak to me like that you young whipper-snapper. I'll have you know, I. . ."

Myra didn't wait for the rest of the tirade. "Oh, go to hell, Mr Mortnel." She slammed the door, turned to face her apartment and burst into uncontrollable tears. The proud part of her wanted to stop crying, yet another part of her wanted to cry and cry and cry until she could dislodge all the unremitting inner pain.

It was not time to act just yet. She had to calm down. She needed to finish the manuscript and to be sure that Anita had read all of it before she did anything; she wanted to know that Anita understood, at least in part, what she was trying to say. Perhaps the unfinished manuscript that she had lent to her friend had been handed to someone else to read; she could not be sure of that, but she had almost completed it; there was not too much more to do. For the moment she must carry on with the everyday matters that everyone else seemed to feel to be so important and yet to her seemed so trivial.

She always kept a box of 'Ultra balm lotioned' tissues on her coffee table and so she went across, took a couple and wiped her eyes. Even these felt dusty against her cheeks. She then went to the bathroom for a quick wash and to dab on a little make-up in order to face the outside world and hide the blotchiness of her skin. She must be strong.

She scrutinised her reflection in the mirror. She did not look strong: she looked tired and gaunt. The beauty of which she had spent a lifetime exploiting seemed to be dissipating in front of her eyes.

At least it wasn't raining outside and she did not need to travel on the bus today. She could get everything she needed at the corner shop; it was more expensive than the supermarket but that didn't matter. It was always a trial getting the pushchair onto the bus, trying to manoeuvre it into the one allocated space without knocking anyone's legs and hoping that no other young mother had grabbed the space before her. People were reluctant to give up their seats, even for someone with a small baby.

Miriam had finally fallen asleep and didn't even stir when Myra manhandled her into her pushchair. The little mite had a slightly seeping dampness around the top of the legs, but she would just have to put up with it. The feeling of dampness could not be that bad as it had certainly not stopped her from falling asleep.

It was not long before Myra and Miriam were traversing the aisles of the corner shop looking for the few odds and ends that were needed.

Myra was not sure if Mrs Mortnel had heard or even seen her leave her apartment and make her way down the road, but there the old lady was in the same shop, shuffling purposefully towards her and baby Miriam.

She really could not understand why Mrs Mortnel always wore patent court shoes; they must be so uncomfortable and Myra always felt that her neighbour wore too much make-up for a woman in her early eighties, but perhaps that was her way of coping with such a domineering husband. Or perhaps her husband insisted that she always dressed befitting the wife of a warrant officer. Myra didn't know and didn't really care. Actually, Mrs Mortnel clearly had a sense of pride in her appearance and in her public persona; Myra admired her for that. In fact, she had tried to give her intended alter ego, Mrs May Kilman, similar traits: both women seemed to have suffered more than their fair share in life.

"Ahh, I am so glad that I have run into you." Mrs Mortnel said as she approached Myra, who in turn truly did not believe that this encounter was in any way coincidental. Neither did she miss the look of disapproval, albeit fleeting, at the ready-made meals Myra had in her basket; the thought of no fresh vegetables must have been an anathema to the 'Healthy Food, Healthy Mind' philosophy of the Warrant Officer's wife. Mrs Mortnel would have been scandalised had she seen Myra's sleight of hand to secrete an extra bar of chocolate in the folds of the hood on her daughter's pushchair. Old habits were hard to break. She did not need to resort to stealing; she just wanted to. She wanted to feel the excitement occasioned by breaking the rules. She did not believe that she was doing anyone any harm. She certainly had no sympathy for the shop owners.

Seemingly oblivious, Mrs Mortnel continued, "I just want to apologise to you on my husband's behalf. You see. . ." and here is where she became a little quieter as if telling Myra something extremely confidential and conspiratorial, "My husband has a heart of gold."

Myra's change of expression from false politeness to sheer incredulity must have unnerved the elderly lady, as she appeared to lose her thread for a moment or two but then she continued. "Oh, he has. He has made a few mistakes in life, but I've forgiven him those." Myra's eyebrows were raised but Mrs Mortnel carried on regardless. "Yes, but that's another matter that I do not need to go into here. A few minor flings before he settled down.

"He isn't very good at being subtle and he really hopes that your bonny little bunny is healthy. He does bluster rather a lot and actually it's not very good for his health but, as the saying goes, 'his bark is worse than his bite'. He means well and I really hope that he has not upset you." She seemed genuinely concerned.

"Rest assured, Mrs Mortnel, my bonny little bunny is healthy."

Mrs Mortnel started giggling like a child, "Oh, did I say 'bunny'; how remiss of me. I meant to say bundle, but bunny suffices well enough, doesn't it? Oh, and do call me Amy. I have said this to you before. I am sure I have previously told you my name on a number of occasions. There really is no need to stand on ceremony."

This lady was so different to her awful husband; they seemed like polar opposites. Myra just could not conceive how they ever got together in the first place, let alone why she married him. She could only imagine and fabricate some chance meeting. That was one thing that Myra did possess in abundance: a vivid imagination. "Thank you Mrs. . . Amy."

Amy Mortnel seemed happy enough with this. She turned away and walked out of the shop. She had not made any purchases whatsoever.

Myra's manuscript notes:

Kilman – dead or alive?
Rethink his attitude to women, especially his wife

Fiction

The Manuscript
Part Nine

Unexpectedly Alive

Rusty Howard stood over the recumbent Kilman. *"How are you feeling, sir?"*

Tentatively, Kilman sat up on the bed and felt a strong searing pain in his chest. He slowly took control of his breathing and looked about the room, gradually taking in the unfamiliar surroundings. He had no idea where he was, but he certainly recognised the man by his side as Mr Russell Howard, the security guard from the government offices. *"Where am I?"*

"Well, sir, you're in a safe house. I was instructed to fetch a dead body from an establishment in the Couple Sector, only to find that the body was not dead after all, sir. It is rare for a dead body to groan, is it not, sir?"

Kilman started to recall his confrontation with his wife. He could remember the terrible headache, then the raised voices, the intense anger and then, without warning, she lunged at him. He could remember no more. *"My wife. . ."*

"Oh, your wife is safe enough. A little upset, sir. She truly believed that she had killed you, but she will be fine. You must admit that she has been sorely tried of late."

Kilman attempted to get himself up into a more upright sitting position, but the pain shot through him. Rusty Howard helped him to sit up more comfortably and then began to explain the circumstances as he perceived them to be. His words were very enlightening.

"I understand, and your wife has confirmed this, that you have been suffering from strong headaches recently. Looking at your company medical records, you have, in fact. always suffered from unaccountable headaches but they have become progressively worse in recent months. Would you say that this is accurate, sir?"

Kilman nodded, too surprised to say anything.

Russell Howard continued: "The tyramine in your system would account for that. You are someone who is prone to headaches but their potency is magnified by the tyramine found in particular drinks and foodstuffs. There are, I'm afraid, some people in our society who, although not wishing to do you any long term harm, would gain some degree of gratification from your discomfort. I believe that you have taken pleasure from a number of illicit liaisons with a woman who participates in what is often referred to as the world's oldest profession. Rudyard Kipling being the originator of that idea, I think, but perhaps I should not admit to that particular snippet of knowledge, and I seem to have digressed from the point.

"This particular lady is very loyal to her customers, yet was persuaded by another, who had become aware of your frequent visits and knowing of your condition, and who informed her that you had a certain penchant for red wine and vintage cheese. This citizen, who had very good personal reasons for despising the Government and who has since suffered more greatly than you as she has lost her life, had an understandable desire to wish any influential government official to experience a little discomfort. Consequently she readily supplied your paramour with the aforementioned food and drink at no cost. Your paramour, unaware of your condition, was more than happy to ply you with red wine and vintage cheese, particularly as it also gave her the opportunity to partake of these luxuries. Unfortunately, although you have a tendency to like cheese and red wine, sir, they don't like you very much. And, of course, you tended to visit your courtesan after work and just before going home, so that you always associated your headaches with home. If you don't mind me saying, but with a little more depth of thought, sir, I think you would have realised that it was not your wife who was the perpetrator of your headaches.

"Then, of course, there was your obsession with the exploits of Mr Silva. Your persistence in trying to find out how he was *interfering with the Elevation Test results irked him to the point that he had to find a way of diverting your attention and so he brought forward, as a temporary measure, the raid on Tania Alexander's home. This gave him time to continue with his clandestine activities. Your 'death' helped him out tremendously."*

"I didn't kill Nina Alexander. I didn't kill her." The despair in Kilman's voice was palpable. He had suddenly realised that she was the one who had supplied the wine and cheese. How she had discovered his affair, he did not know, but she would have enjoyed nothing better than to make such a highly ranked government officer pay the price for his indiscretions.

"Tania's mother?"

"Yes, I didn't kill her."

"I know, sir. She killed herself. You had no reason to kill her. She killed herself rather than let Mr Silva see her watch the authorities take away her child. There is some history there of which you are unaware and of which there is no need to explain in great detail at this point. She poisoned herself, but your recent aggressive behaviour made you the prime suspect with regard to the possible cause of her death."

Kilman had the good grace to redden. He dropped his gaze in shame. "Does my wife know about all of this?"

"Yes, she does, sir, but she would like to spend some time with you to talk things through. To think about the future; not only your future together, if I may say, but the future of the young people of Lithport."

Kilman raised his head and looked at Rusty Howard with immense intensity. The words flowed from his lips, "They're sent away. No child is ever put to death. You must believe me."

"Oh, I do, sir, and I know. You do not believe that I have worked all my life for the government not to have realised that, but we need to think about what to do about Mr Silva, sir, as I am sure you will agree. He is not as he appears to be. His mind has become rather wild of late and, not to put it too bluntly, sir, he must be stopped."

"I do not understand what he is doing. Surely the system as it stands is ideal." The arrogant tone was still there.

"Ideal?"

"It works, Mr Howard." Kilman could not bring himself to call this man by his first name: a man who had worked for so many

years, supposedly as a caretaker, who clearly possessed greater knowledge than he was accredited with by Kilman himself if not by others. "Every child of a certain age is tested. Those with potential are nurtured either here or elsewhere."

"Only males are nurtured here, sir, and the females are sent away. And how convenient that the rumours abound that they are eliminated so that there are no issues with regard to family ties and having to keep in touch. Once at their allocated destination they are 'nurtured' as you say, but their roots are forgotten as if they never existed. And this is 'ideal'?" Rusty Howard's tone of voice clearly indicated that he did not agree with Kilman's clinical assessment.

Kilman had never questioned himself in this way. His own inability to show emotion had coloured his views towards others.

Rusty Howard continued, "You do realise that we have recently discovered that Silva's own daughter resides in the area outside The Wall?" He looked at the genuine surprise in Kilman's eyes. "No, clearly you did not."

"Presumably he wanted to keep in touch with her."

"Originally we believed this to be the case, but this has become a little more doubtful in recent times and we are unsure with regard to his intentions. We believe that her life is at risk."

"His intentions?"

"Yes, Mr Kilman. We believe, sir, that Mr Silva intends to kill those who reside outside The Wall in one dramatic wave of violence."

Kilman was incredulous, "When? And how many are there outside The Wall?"

"Oh, we are not entirely sure, sir, but we are keeping a close eye on proceedings and we'll keep you closely informed, don't you worry about that. I believe that Mr Silva had the capacity to bribe the worker responsible for the vehicular transition of young female Elevationists from Lithport to their next doctrinal destination."

"You describe the next stage of their training as 'doctrinal', Mr Howard?"

"Yes, sir, I do and if truth be known, I think that the whole system needs to be addressed, but that is for greater powers than I. For the moment, we are dealing with the here and now."

Kilman felt suitably humbled. "Who are 'we', Mr Howard?"

"Well, there's Lisa Watts and there's my team, but I think it's time you saw your wife, sir. She has been waiting patiently for quite some time."

And with that, Rusty Howard left the room to fetch Mrs May Kilman.

Tania and Kim: New Friends

Tania and Kim sat together in the kitchen area. The other girls had left to spend their time usefully in and around the complex: gardening, doing general repairs, clearing ground for further building projects.

"You seem very worried, Kim." Tania had wanted to find a moment alone with the usually bubbly young woman whose friendship she had been deliberately nurturing over the past weeks. She lost no time in introducing the subject that concerned her. "And I am convinced that you're worried about Mary."

Kim cradled her fruit drink between her two hands and looked down at the rippling pale pink liquid as if to find inspiration. "This is not right. . . not right at all." A deep sigh escaped from her inner being as she turned her face upwards towards her friend. "This beautiful place in which we all live should be a haven of happiness and fulfilment, but it's just not right."

Tania said nothing. She allowed the thoughts of her companion to develop and form into something tangible.

Kim spoke again, but this time she looked Tania in the eye and her tone was more matter-of-fact with its forced control. "You do know that Mary is Silva's daughter. He prepared this place for her. He knew I would join her; I have been her close friend for years. We grew up together. Practically in each other's pockets, if we were permitted to have pockets that is. Pockets allow us to hide things, to be secretive, but of course you know that.

"This place was to be a kind of safe house, I suppose, where we could not be reached and taken away never to be seen or heard of again. Silva is due to retire from the Government soon, you know, and then he will come here to be with us. Or more precisely, to be with his daughter. Or, at least, that was the plan."

She paused and looked gravely at Tania. "But it's his attitude. He cannot hide his attitude, however much he might try. Does he strike you as someone desperate to join his daughter?"

134

Tania shook her head, but remained silent. The question was rhetorical; she knew that more needed to be said.

Indeed, Kim continued, "If he didn't want to see her anymore, surely he should have let her have the Elevation Test and then say his goodbyes. Perhaps, at first, he did want to be with her; to find a way to be with her. Possibly he felt a sense of responsibility to his late wife and then he realised that he felt nothing for his daughter. I just don't really understand him, but I do know that I am afraid. She desperately wants his love, and all I can see is disappointment and. . . fear. Yes, she's afraid of him and, yes I am worried, Tania, and I really do not know what to do. I am more worried as the time for his retirement seems to be getting closer and closer."

Tania realised that even this revelation was not the full story, but Kim was now lost in her own personal reverie and that was all she would divulge for the time being. Tania feared that time was a luxury they did not truly possess. A number of ideas, not as yet fully developed, were forming in her mind and had been for a few days. She knew that she had to do something. Time was pressing. "Is there any way I can get back to Lithport without anyone knowing? Perhaps you could tell everyone here that I am not well and you have decided that the best thing for me is to be in bed out of everyone's way until I recover. Say that I should not have any visitors, as I am too ill.

"I think that the time has come for me to return to the township. I have a few questions that I want to ask and it is only there that I will find the answers. I think that I have an idea about what is going on. Will you help? I truly believe we will all benefit from this if I can get back."

With some reluctance, Kim agreed to help. She was, understandably, very nervous about the safety of the compound's newest recruit to whom she had grown very attached. How would she know that Tania was safe once she had left? She would never forgive herself if something happened to her. She also wondered what this seemingly guileless sylph-like girl could possibly achieve. In the end, she realised that, however small and fragile she appeared on the outside, Tania was a determined young being who would not be diverted from this course of action: not even with the offer of her favourite home baked biscuits! After receiving assurances that she would be back within two days and, as a mischievous addendum, an understanding that not all members of the safe house were as isolated as she had been led to believe, Kim acquiesced. Tania was fully aware that Kim would be able to track her movements and know of her whereabouts. It was agreed that the departure would take place immediately.

Kim duly accompanied Tania to the front of the safe house and helped her remove the camouflage cloth and vegetation from the auto-bikes. The two of them fell into a warm embrace before Tania pulled herself away, alighted one of the bikes and started the small engine. She recognised its purring sound, but this time it lacked the comforting feel that it had before. Kim moved back as much of the vegetation as she could and quietly whispered, "Good luck." She stood and watched as Tania rode away.

Tania sped over the terrain, taking as direct a route as she could back to The Wall. Plants reached out with their stinging tendrils and malicious thorns, scratching her legs as she rode past. She took no notice. Her joyous feelings from the natural breeze that had flowed through her hair when she had first arrived here had dissipated; this time her eyes watered from the cold air, adding a misty film to the way ahead of her. Twice she fell to the ground, and twice she got up and went on her way. The auto-bike was heavier than she had anticipated but she managed and it was not long before The Wall loomed above her head before her.

For some reason she suddenly recalled the conversation she had had about godparents and their belief in a transcendental being guiding them through life. "Well God, if you do exist, you need to guide me now."

Within seconds, God answered.

There immediately in front of her was the doorway to The Wall and into Lithport.

Reality

Chapter Ten

Old Tricks

Boy did she need that. The night had certainly boosted her self-esteem. Perhaps she had not lost her sex appeal after all. A teacher too. She was definitely going up in the world: not a dusty caretaker or a self-centred, self-satisfied and self-important body-builder or a car engineer smelling of oil, but a teacher.

She tried to direct the key into its allotted slot but for some reason she kept missing. Then the door just opened as if by magic. "Hello Myra," came the smiling voice of Anita, who had been more than happy to do some babysitting for the evening, especially when the meeting was so important. Myra had told her friend that she was meeting up with a new agent who could get her work published. She was not happy with the present agent who did not seem to be making any effort for her.

This was not exactly the truth, but a little subterfuge never did any harm. She had no intention of meeting a new agent. There was no need. Admittedly the old one had started to feel guilty; it seemed that he and his wife were getting on better now and he wanted to thank Myra for that. She had reinvigorated his sex drive. His wife was pregnant, so 'getting on better' had clearly taken on a new meaning. Apparently he now needed to reassess his priorities.

Myra had never believed him, anyway, when he vowed he loved her and would do anything for her, including leaving his wife. As far as she was concerned, men were useful for one thing, and one thing only, and he had done nothing to change her mind. When she returned to her apartment, she herself felt reinvigorated, but it had very little, if anything, to do with procuring a new agent.

Anita had been sitting in the front room watching a late night television programme. The volume was down low as she did not want to disturb Miriam; it also enabled her to hear Myra's inept attempts at gaining entry to her own apartment. She greeted her warmly with a heavy dose of sarcasm. "Successful meeting?"

She was then left to close the door as Myra brushed past her with a confident wave of her arm. "Oh yes, it was really successful. I have to send him some of my work and he'll assess what he sees as my potential. I pointed him in the direction of stuff I've had published in the past. He seemed happy. I will be meeting up with him again in about two weeks' time. Nice chap." Having finished her prepared speech, she broached the subject that was of greater interest to her.

"Talking of meeting up with people. I was introduced to a teacher from your school the other day. James Coburn I think his name was. Teaches history."

"You sure it was as long ago as the other day? How about earlier this evening?" Anita gave an artful smile.

Myra looked at her and laughed. "You knew. You knew all the time."

"Just an intelligent guess. He told me at work today that he had a date this evening. Now what was the girl's name? Oh yes, I remember." There was a deliberate pause, followed by a sardonic tone, "Avis Marly. What sort of name is that! Other than conveniently being an anagram of Myra Vilas?"

Myra plonked herself rather heavily onto the sofa. "Seriously Anita, he was telling me about the new Head of Department post coming up at your place. He thinks you should apply. I agree. You deserve promotion; you work really hard." She leaned forward, focusing her slightly hazy and inebriated attention on her friend's face. "I want you to promise you'll apply."

Anita's self-doubt surfaced and she became more solemn. "Oh, I don't know. I've thought about it, but it would just be loads more hassle for very little extra money. I can do without more hassle. There is so much about the school's learning policies that I just don't agree with. If I get promotion, I'm advocating their ideas."

"No you're not. You're just making excuses. Don't be so damned weak. You can only change thongs from the inside."

"Thongs!"

"Oh, things, things, things! You know I meant to say 'things'. I'm being serious, Anita."

Internally, Anita wavered between walking over to Myra and either hugging her tightly to show her understanding that her friend truly cared for her or knocking her off the sofa for being such a pain. She was not quite sure which to do, but rightly or wrongly decided to divert the present topic elsewhere and possibly touch someone else's Achilles Heel. "I know. I'll think about it. Now, changing the subject to someone more dear to my heart. Miriam was really good this evening. She's such a beauty, Myra."

Myra gave a vague smile but made no comment. She pointed in the general direction of her cabinet. "The last bit of the manuscript is over there, in the drawer. The denu. . . denow. . . den. . . something or other."

"Denouement?" Anita suggested.

"That's the one. Just take it and read it."

Anita went over to the drawer and did as requested. She turned; Myra had fallen asleep. Anita put the manuscript on to the coffee table. She clumsily manoeuvred a mumbling Myra out of the room into her bedroom; let her lie down on the bed; took off her shoes; carefully placed the duvet over her and left the room. She took one last look at her friend; a brief glance in on Miriam to check that she was fine; and then quietly left the apartment, collecting the manuscript on her way out.

An inexplicable but deep-rooted sadness seemed to overwhelm her. Myra had deserved to have a break; she deserved to have a good evening, but to totally ignore her daughter was unbearable to Anita. She drove home as a lone tear slowly meandered down her cheek.

Fiction

The Manuscript
Part Ten

The Denouement

The Corridors of Power

This young girl was unbelievably stealthy. Never before had he allowed anyone to get this far into the building without taking intervenient action. He tried to follow every move on the screen. She seemed to instinctively know where the cameras were; she held her body close to the walls as she moved silently down the corridors. There were brief periods when he lost her completely. She appeared to melt seamlessly into her surroundings.

This was definitely a job for Lisa, whom he knew was in one of the nearby offices. He immediately contacted her. "Lisa. There's a young girl in the building. I think that you might have to intercept. I am not entirely sure who she is or, indeed, where she has come from, although I can hazard a guess on both counts. I decided not to intervene but she appears to be making her way towards the top corridor."

Lisa's response was calm: almost as if she had expected this call. "Okay. I'll follow it up."

Although her voice had appeared outwardly controlled and impassive on the phone, inward nervous anticipation permeated her whole being. She made her way as quickly as she could toward the top corridor. Tania saw her before she saw Tania. "Aunt Lisa!"

Lisa took her in to her arms. "Good stage whisper, Tania." After their heartfelt embrace, she held the young girl at arms'

someone had clumsily tried to hide. These proved relatively easy to follow. They both had such fun manoeuvring the bikes through the wooded area that they had to remind themselves of the seriousness of their task.

It was not long before they reached their destination. Their purpose was to get all the girls to move as far away from the undercover building as they could. They had no idea as to the amount of time they had so it was imperative that the evacuation from the compound took place as soon as possible. Most of the girls had been there for many months; some had been there for years and all of them considered it to be home. Both the evacuation and its urgency were greeted with suspicion and a number of girls vowed that they would not budge.

A few of the girls looked to Mary for guidance and leadership but she remained silent throughout. It was Kim who finally persuaded the community of the need to do as they were asked. It was Kim who organised all of them into smaller groups with specific tasks and areas to check. It was Kim who effectively and efficiently oversaw the whole evacuation procedure.

The Corridors of Power: The Encounter

Tania stepped tentatively over the threshold of Silva's office. He spoke without looking up, "Yes."

She stood there and stared at him until he finally lifted his head.

"Oh, Tania. I didn't expect to see you. I thought you would stay at the safe house."

Her riposte was simple. "Why?"

He knew her question was not a response to his comment; he knew that she was aware of his plans to destroy the forests outside The Wall. Their eyes met, and for a few moments, neither of them said a word. The silence embraced them. He then explained all, knowing that within a very short time it would not matter. She would not be in the forest as he had hoped she would be, but he could easily overpower this small, vulnerable being standing audaciously in front of him. She would not be able to escape and he could easily get rid of her body on the next journey out of the township.

Instinctively Tania realised his thoughts and took a step back towards the door, but she had no intention of leaving until she had some answers.

His harsh feelings softened as he remembered and talked about his wife. "I loved my wife. I never loved another woman, and never will. I knew she had a quality that no one else could ever possess. She was beautiful, but more than that, her sense of calm embraced all who ever came into contact with her. Your demeanour reminds me of her to some degree; nothing really fazes you does it Tania? When my wife died, the world died with her. Or it should have done. Why didn't it? Why did the world remain? Why did people carry on with their lives as if nothing had happened?

"At first everyone avoided me. They didn't know what to say. Then when they felt that the time was right, they patted me on the shoulders, they said they were sorry for my loss. My loss. . ." He paused and looked angrily towards Tania. "I did not lose her. She left me. She allowed death to take her into its welcoming arms. She wanted me to love our child, the monster that had forced her to leave me. People tell me that children are innocent. No. They are not. Children manipulate us, turn our lives upside down. I could never look at that child without hatred in my heart; she was responsible and had to pay. I could have killed her there and then, but I wanted vengeance. I wanted vengeance on a world that did not understand. I wanted all children to die. There was no future for me and I wanted there to be no future for any one ever again. I wanted to destroy this whole ridiculous world in which we live and now I am ready to do exactly that."

His voice, by this stage, had risen to a crescendo, but he took a deep breath and seemed to control his emotions before speaking more quietly. His tone was sinister. "It will not be long now and the society outside of these walls will be obliterated forever and no one will be able to do anything about it. Not even you, my clever empathetic little Tania. Not anybody."

Silva paused and deliberately collected himself. He breathed heavily and let his shoulders gradually become less tense. "I had a lot to do, but I needed people to believe in me. I needed people to think that I could embrace the art of forgiveness as a form of recovery. It was no secret that I blamed the staff, both human and android, for the death of my wife. RECOVERY! How can you recover when your whole world, everything you have ever lived for, is destroyed? People need to know how that feels."

144

"What about the society within The Wall, Mr Silva?"

"Oh, that will also be destroyed, Tania. It will self-destruct. As soon as the men and women out there on the streets find they have no leaders and no children, they will turn upon each other like monsters. They will destroy each other until not a soul remains."

"But there are leaders here Mr Silva. The community will continue."

"You really do not understand, do you, Tania. Kilman is dead; killed by his pathetic little wife. She did me a service. She found a solution for me. He watched me; he suspected me, but not anymore. And as for that Sir Charles Bartholomew-Spence. . ." Silva started to laugh, almost hysterically. He stopped abruptly.

"I have closed all communications with the outside world. This is a temporary measure but it will give me enough time to complete my task. No one will realise the annihilation of this miniature community in which we live until it is too late. No, not live. . . exist. . . until it is too late. I and I alone am the leader of this piteous society and, of course, that means that I am also in control of the Special Services; they answer to me and only me. I have ordered the Special Service Patrols to destroy all the laboratories in the building and arrest all the technicians who, of course, were plotting against the very fabric of our wonderful society. And if anyone should resist, he or she must be eliminated in the name of humanity. Perhaps I should arrange for the same to occur in the Health and Well-being Centre. What do you think, Tania? Lost your tongue?

"Well, no worries. Shall I obliterate that precious community outside The Wall now or shall I wait until more young girls can join you and your new friends? You can watch me, Tania. Here is the button: the button that will send the military air-drones out to destroy every living creature outside The Wall. To think that the stupid Commissioner and his cronies wanted to decommission my beautiful machines." He softly caressed the button without putting any pressure on it.

Circumstances had made this man become totally unreasonable. He was insane. Because he had been hurt during his lifetime, he had an enormous unquenchable desire to hurt all around him. He had never suffered harm or failure during his young life and when

145

g

he became an adult, he was unable to cope with it. The cruel streak within him had given him a kind of fatal arrogance. As long as he was successful in life, all was well, but he did not possess the kind of nature that could cope with adversity.

Tania soon realised that it was futile to try to reason with him, but she made one last attempt. "Please don't do this Mr Silva."

He smiled. Even under such formidable and intimidating circumstances, there she stood: a calm, non-judgemental child. For she was just a child and yet there was such maturity; in the future, she could be a frightening young lady. He would ensure that she would not have a future. "Oh, I am going to do it, perhaps not now, but I am going to, my little Tania, and there is absolutely nothing you can do about it."

She turned and left the room. He was beyond recovery. She could not save him. Now was the time to concentrate on others.

Her first task was to find Lisa as quickly as she possibly could and let her know what Silva had said. They had to stop him. Her next task was to return to the community outside The Wall and do whatever she could to save them.

An overwhelming sense of demonic euphoria took hold of Silva as he lifted his arm high and then dramatically pointed his finger down towards the button that was going to end the lives of all those girls. Slowly and deliberately, his finger descended upon the button and he ended the manoeuvre with a grand flourish of his arm back upwards as if he were the conductor of a large orchestra.

Task accomplished! The button was pressed. The sound of unstoppable and deadly air-drones roared above the township of Lithport.

Silva spoke aloud as if the young girl was still there, even though he knew that she had gone. He did not care anymore. "You know, Tania, I expected more than this. I have waited for so long. I have planned for so long. I expected stronger feelings. A sense of jubilation. No matter. I have accomplished all that I set out to do and no one was able to stop me."

He sat at his desk, silently congratulating himself over his success and taking a welcome sip of the whisky that he had set aside for the occasion as the world outside Lithport became a wasteland of debris: the result of total and utter destruction.

A cursory glance towards the door was all that was needed when he sensed the presence of another visitor: a visitor whom he assumed would be Captain Holmes, the Head of Military Manoeuvres. He believed Captain Holmes to be a man after his own heart and that he was there to tell him that all was complete and his instructions had been carried out successfully. But it wasn't Captain Holmes. The person standing in the doorframe before him was a woman: a woman he knew very well. Lisa Watts.

She only needed one attempt. Her aim was impeccable. She was surprised at how easy it had been: a slight pressure on the trigger, a minor jolt and Silva slumped back slowly into his chair. The laser beam had been devastatingly effective. She had not expected any blood but was momentarily fascinated by a tiny trickle of viscous red fluid that eased its way from his mouth, down his chin.

Her voice was one of authority. "Captain!"

A tall uniformed man appeared immediately behind her. "Ma'am?"

"You can now give all of your patrols clearance to leave the city and search for signs of life outside The Wall. And if you have done as ordered, replacing the R2 Explosive Devices with benign sound bombs and altering the course of the military air-drones, the harmless detonations should have taken place over barren, uninhabited areas. There should be many signs of life, I believe. In fact, there should be no casualties whatsoever. The only casualty is Raymond A. N. Silva. Am I right in this belief, Captain Holmes?"

"Yes ma'am." Captain Holmes also seemed to be momentarily distracted by the lifeless body in front of him, before continuing: "All machine loads were replaced with sound bombs. We manually altered the destination course but, as discussed previously, Mr Silva had the capacity to override this aspect."

"Yes, I am aware of that, Captain, and this is why we sent out reconnaissance for transitional manoeuvres to ensure zero loss of life. Good work, Captain."

"Thank you, ma'am." Captain Holmes smiled and turned to leave whilst shouting further orders to his subordinate waiting in the corridors to put the next military step into action.

Lisa Watts took one more disdainful look at Silva. She felt nothing.

Outside The Wall: The Aftermath

One hour later, almost fifty young women were recovered from an underground community. Almost fifty. One was missing.

Kim, her tear-stained face betraying the agonies of her desperate and fruitless search for her childhood friend, saw Tania approaching and rushed over to her. "I can't find Mary. We were instructed to evacuate and I thought she was with me. Then came the blasts. It was so frightening. One minute she was there and the next she was gone. It was all so manic and loud. Some of the girls were screaming and everyone was rushing about in different directions. I really don't know where she is. I need to go back."

Tania placed her hands calmly but firmly onto Kim's arms and looked into her eyes with an assuredness that was exceptional for one so young. "No. You look after the girls. Ensure that they are all safe and accounted for. They will listen to you, Kim. I'll find Mary."

Tania made her way back to the safe house as swiftly as she could and as quickly as the broken terrain would allow. She clambered over rubble and on more than one occasion stumbled over the rugged ground, grazing her legs on the edges of rocks and stones. Every footstep seemed to kick up a constrictive cloud of dust, further hampering her progress. She stopped for a moment to tie a small handkerchief around her mouth in an attempt to protect herself as much as she could. It seemed to take forever to get back but she managed it. She automatically made her way to Mary's own apartment room. The door was locked.

"Mary! Mary! It's Tania. You need to come with me." She knew Mary was in there, yet she also realised that she couldn't open the door by herself. She looked around frantically for something to break the door down, but there was no way that she had the strength to do that.

Then she remembered. Kim had told her that she kept a spare key in the kitchen area. She rushed to the kitchen, spun around mumbling, "Where? Where? Where?" She opened drawers and cupboards; looked under cushions; and swept her arm along the work surfaces. And then, there it was: a caricature, a child's plaything. The teddy bear. The key to Mary's room was sellotaped inside a plastic wallet at the base of the biscuit barrel.

148

Tania rushed back and unlocked the door. Mary had constructed a noose which she hung from a beam in the ceiling. She stood on a chair with her head in the noose and just as Tania entered the room, Mary kicked the chair away.

Finally Making the Connection

Lisa Watts reached into her pocket for her clandestine government issue mobile, which was immediately answered before she even heard a single ringing tone.

"Yes."

"The target has been terminated, sir."

"Any collateral damage?"

"None."

"And the air-drones were neutralised as commanded?"

"Yes, sir."

"Has Captain Holmes been given permission to search outside The Wall for signs of life?"

"He has, sir. We know that Mr and Mrs Kilman managed to get to the girls in good time so we are not expecting any fatalities and if there are any injuries, they should only be minor ones."

"Good work, Ms Watts, I am very proud of all that you have done." He paused. "What about the young girl?"

Lisa turned. Tania had found her immediately after the failed discussion with Silva, so she knew that she was safe. However, since then Lisa had been so caught up in everything that she had to do that she had not exactly forgotten about Tania with all the activity that had taken place but she had assumed, wrongly it would seem, that the girl must have followed her. She hadn't. Lisa sighed deeply. "She seems to have gone, sir."

There was no violent reaction from the other end. "I think we can both hazard a calculated guess regarding her whereabouts. I am sure you know what to do. Leave Captain Holmes to get any mess outside The Wall cleared up. I am sure that Mr Howard will also help wherever necessary. Hopefully we have no casualties to deal with. Once again, congratulations on your success. You are now in charge. Welcome on board, you are the new Head of Government and Societal Communication of Lithport. I look forward to us working together, just as we have done over the past months, but now it can all be official."

Lisa smiled, "Yes, sir." This may not have been the right time to start indicating how she would embark upon enforcing her new powers, but she ventured her ideas anyway. "And I would like to start by stopping any movement of young girls from this fine township to other township training facilities. We have all the expertise we need here and we can nurture our own citizens. The people of Lithport have lived in fear for too long."

What the reaction was to that, she did not discover. The mobile signal had gone dead, but she imagined that Sir Arthur Bartholomew-Spence would support her unequivocally in all her efforts to create an equal society.

Our World?

Kilman needed to check that all the girls had managed to escape from the safe house. Like Tania, he had also gone back to search for Mary, leaving his wife with the remainder of the evacuees. He had not been far behind Tania when she returned from speaking with Kim, but he was slower in his pursuit.

When he arrived at the compound, he helped Tania to get Mary down and between the two of them they had been able to quickly transport her back to Lithport and into the Health and Well-being Centre. Her life was now out of their hands; they could do nothing more.

Tania waited in the corridor for news, and when she saw Kim emerge from Mary's private room, she rushed towards her. "Is she going to be okay?"

"Yes. She's asleep now, but she'll be fine. You know, she's pregnant. And Silva's the father." The anger started to build. "Her own father raped her. He lost his temper with her. He came to visit her and she asked and asked and asked when he was going to retire and live in the safe house that he had created. He gently caressed her, told her that she reminded him of her mother. His caresses became firmer and firmer, his eyes became harsher and harsher. Mary was scared and he raped her. How could he? His own child? He never had any intention of joining us at the safe house. It was all pretence to get us there and then destroy us. He's a monster."

"Was a monster. Silva is dead." They both turned on hearing the voice of Lisa Watts. Neither of them had noticed her arrive.

150

"We all have a new life to look forward to and with support from the two of you, Mary will be part of that new life."

A Note from the Author

We are faced with a myriad of possible futures; this is only one of them.

Tania was one child in this myriad of possible futures. She had received no meaningful contact from her father: he was taken away from her before he had even had the chance to hold her in his arms. She did not become pregnant, she did not become a criminal and it cannot be said that she felt disadvantaged. She had a loving mother who was prepared to die for her.

Mary was one child in this myriad of possible futures. Her loving mother died the day she was born. She had a father but received no meaningful contact from him: he abused his responsibilities as a parent. He abandoned his love for her the day she was born. She was left bereft. He deserved to die.

I say to those postulatory experts of 2013: the poverty of which you should be concerned cannot be calculated in billions of pounds each year. You have totally missed the point. Poverty is not engendered by lack of money or having only one parent. One parent alone, male or female, can provide so much love and care that a second parent is not a prerequisite. But if that love is abused, if that one parent does not have the capacity to carry out this so important duty of care then he, or indeed she, must face the consequences. Being forced to live with an abusive or inadequate parent is a life sentence no child should ever have to endure; that is poverty of the most heinous type.

'A Parallel Life' is a work of fiction, but it is a work of fiction in which realities can be found.

The End

Reality

Chapter Eleven

Myra's de die in diem

After yet another night with very little sleep, the exhausted fledgling mother opened the door to her friend, Anita, who held out a ream of stapled papers. "Well, I got some bits right! Really good read. Sorry, I can't stay, but I've got to get to work. Mind you, it sounds as though you have your hands full anyway." Then she paused, scrutinising more closely the usually immaculate and beautiful young woman standing on the threshold of her apartment. "God, you look awful. What on earth is the matter?"

The plaintive cries of Myra's baby could be heard from the back room. "Oh. Little Miriam's just been an absolute nightmare over the past few days. I've been up all night with her and Corporal Dead Ringer keeps coming around complaining about the noise. Miriam is obviously teething. I can't seem to do anything with her. But we'll get through it." She added a weak smile almost as an afterthought.

Anita was totally unconvinced by this display of nonchalance, especially as in the background she could see a pile of clothes thrown haphazardly on to the floor: this was not the Myra she knew. However, she had to get to work. She had made this visit during an end of morning free period and she should really still be at school. Something inside, a gut feeling, had urged her to see Myra at a time that she would not normally descend upon her friend; returning a copy of the manuscript seemed to be a good reason to drop by unannounced. She didn't really want to leave her visit until the evening as she had actually made other arrangements for that particular evening. She now needed to get back to work as she suddenly realised that she had arranged to meet up with a handful of pupils from her tutor group during the lunch break so that they could do any necessary last minute alterations for their afternoon assembly on anti-bullying. In addition to this she had to check that the technicians had connected up the computer in the hall to relay the large visual display; and she wanted to ensure that her classroom was ready for the final afternoon's lesson on 'The Tempest'. The list of jobs to do was seemingly endless.

But she was unhappy; rather than feeling relieved by the visit, she felt even more strongly that something was decidedly wrong.

She smiled sympathetically towards Myra and turned away as the door closed behind her and, right on cue, 'Corporal Dead Ringer' strode up to her. "Infernal noise. She can't even control her own child. Single mother, of course. She should live with those other single mothers down Stoneharbour Lane. This used to be a quiet block. How she could afford an upmarket place like this, I'll never know." Anita could feel the venom with which he spat out his words. "Don't know how she got a place like this. Pleaded poverty and got benefits of some kind or other. Some rich relative perhaps, just to keep her quiet and out of the way."

Anita didn't bother to tell him that Myra's father had paid for the apartment: a father whom she never saw. She attempted a look of understanding and went on her way. She did not have the time to stand there and argue.

Warrant Officer Mortnel stood in no-man's-land for a few seconds and then made his way back to his own apartment. At the threshold, waiting for him, stood an eighty-one year old world weary woman; she had seen it all before.

Anita's World

It had been a long, tedious hour but at last the time was approaching for the bell that indicated the end of the lesson and Anita needed to bring the session to a close. She had to admit that she had not taught her best lesson to date. Differentiation, competent classroom management and behaviour management would probably be given 'Needs Improvement' or whatever phrase was presently in vogue for the school inspectors and the pompous members of the School Leadership Team, whose own rare teaching episodes probably 'Needed Improvement' if truth be known. She was certainly not in the right frame of mind to inspire her students today and it was not particularly surprising that her Year 11 class seemed to lack interest in the romantic aspect of Shakespeare's 'The Tempest'; romance was an uncomfortable subject for fifteen and sixteen year olds at the best of times. But at least they weren't 'climbing the walls', as the saying goes.

"So today we have reviewed the initial meeting of Ferdinand and Miranda in Act 1 Scene 2 of 'The Tempest'. And next lesson I would like us to spend more time thinking about their relationship in the play where Ferdinand refers to Miranda as 'Admir'd Miranda'."

A hand shot up.

"Yes Aaron?"

"Is it an anagram, Miss?"

A voice full of impatient frustration interjected from the back of the classroom, "Shut up, Aaron, it's the end of the lesson. Stop asking stupid questions. Some of us want to get home."

"No it's okay Suzie, it's not quite time for the bell and it's a relevant question. If you look at the letters of the two words, you will see that there is only one 'a' in the word 'Admir'd' but two in the name 'Miranda'. However, the general opinion is that Shakespeare is deliberately playing with the name he has created for this female character."

Suzie's response was to shout out in the cruellest of tones she could muster, "Yay! You got it wrong Smarty Knickers." At which point she did a very unconvincing whining imitation of her schoolmate, "Is it an anagram, Miss?"

The immediate volcano of laughter from the rest of the class clearly indicated that there was little point in trying to continue. Anita also decided to employ what she referred to as selective eyesight and ignore Aaron's raised finger directed at Suzie towards the back of the room. She clapped her hands loudly, raised her voice and gradually gained control. "Just stand behind your chairs everyone and we'll wait for the b. . ."

At which point there was a screeching, howling racket

154

recognised by all as the school bell indicating the end of the lesson and, indeed, the end of the school day.

For once she didn't worry that none of her students actually waited to be formally dismissed. They just left, with one or two of them wishing their teacher a good weekend. Generally, however, none of them harboured any serious thoughts whatsoever about the woman who had calmly talked them through the authenticity of love at first sight on an island that may or may not have been in the Mediterranean. It was the weekend; they had their own lives to concentrate on for two full days.

For all they knew or cared, their teacher of English might just as well lock herself in a school cupboard and not emerge again until Monday morning in order to teach them. Surely she did not have a life outside the school premises?

Friday Evening

Anita scrolled down all the available TV channels. Friday evening's selection of programmes was totally uninspiring. In the end, she decided on 'Mock the Week'; it was probably a repeat but it was usually pretty amusing. She was feeling irritated that her prior engagement had been cancelled at the last minute and she was left alone to entertain herself. She felt slightly cheated. It was not the most exciting start to the weekend. She debated internally as to whether she should visit Myra: if she dropped by unannounced again, her friend would certainly be suspicious.

The television programme came to life as Dara Ó Briain was introducing a round entitled 'Picture of the Week' which depicted Theresa May just leaving number ten Downing Street and waving to the journalists across the street. There were a few humorous comments about the prime minister's nickname being Submarine, due to her supposed tendency to disappear whenever there were difficult issues to deal with, and then Hugh Dennis, in his indomitable way, interjected with, "Did you know that 'hate my arse' is an anagram of Theresa May?" Anagrams really did seem to be a dominant feature of Anita's day.

Her mind started to wander. Not surprisingly, her musings returned to Myra, her daughter, the manuscript, recent comments; the one that suddenly sprung to mind was, "I enjoy playing with words, especially people's names." Even the final words of the manuscript played on her mind, 'It is a work of fiction in which realities can be found.'

The audience laughter on 'Mock the Week' melted into the background as Anita's thoughts turned away from the television celebrities' antics to more immediate concerns.

Reality and fiction started to merge together, "An anagram. . . a play on words. . . of course. What an idiot I've been. . ." A tumble of names permeated her mind:

"*Silva*. . .Vilas; *Alice*. . .Celia; *Mary*. . .Myra." Then there was "*May*. . .Amy." And more personally significant, "*Tania*. . .Anita." Every single one of them was an anagram. Even Nina was an anagram of her own mother's name Anni. How did Myra know her mother's name? And how did she know that no one ever put the e on the end because that was how she had always spelt her name as a child and it stuck with her throughout her life.

Episodes in the manuscript became clearer, more poignant; characters became real people; fictional events allied themselves to reality. Parallel lives: parallel worlds. She had not solved the puzzle at all as she had previously claimed, but now she was beginning to do so.

The strength of her impulse to contact Myra could not be ignored. She reached across to her mobile phone, "Come on, Myra. Answer. Answer!"

All the while she held the mobile to her ear but there was no reply.

Getting to Myra's apartment became her number one priority. Fortunately the glass of wine that she had poured herself earlier in the evening remained untouched. She went to the door, took the bunch of keys from the hook beneath the mirror and rushed out into the night.

She drove with care, albeit a little more speedily than usual, whilst desperately wanting to get to her friend's as soon as she could. Why was it that the slowest driver in the whole universe always materialised in front of her whenever she wanted to get somewhere quickly: whenever she was running late for school, a doctor's appointment or an important meeting? Throughout the whole journey she was cursing herself for not having realised sooner: the manuscript was a complex and enigmatic message. She could not fully unravel its various strands at the moment but she knew not all augured well.

Before she had even turned the corner, she detected a change in the traffic, a subtle deceleration as if there was something ahead worth slowing down for. As she turned the corner, she saw the lights. She saw the ambulance. She knew it was for Myra.

She pulled up as close as she could and rushed from the car. Locking it didn't seem to be a priority. She flew towards where two ambulance men were carrying the stretcher with Myra on it. "Myra! Myra!"

And then she realised that the person on the stretcher was a man, not a woman. It was Warrant Officer Mortnel. But the sight of the stretcher had made her panic; she could not think straight; she started screaming, "But what about Myra and the baby?" The usual calm persona had gone.

A policeman stopped her abruptly. "Excuse me, ma'am, there is nothing to see here. You need to go on your way."

"But it's the woman in the next flat who's in danger. Have you seen her? Is her baby alright? Are they both still alive?"

The policeman, not surprisingly, had no idea about whom she was talking. However, he remained quiet but firm. "The gentleman has had a heart attack; there is no woman involved. As you can see, his wife is with him. There's nothing for you to worry about, ma'am."

"But there is. You don't understand."

She pushed past the policeman who had been momentarily distracted by the sound of an impatient driver competently demonstrating that he had not forgotten how to use his car horn. She rushed over to Mrs Mortnel who was holding her husband's hand and smiling down at him as he desperately tried to speak to her. "I'm sorry, May. I'm so sorry. I love you so much. I've been such an idiot."

"Now don't you go fretting any more, dear. Everything will be alright."

Amy Mortnel then became aware of Anita. "Oh, hello dear. We've just had a little situation here."

A little situation! How could she be so unflustered by this? "Oh, Mrs Mortnel, I'm so sorry. I just saw the ambulance and I thought it was for Myra."

Amy Mortnel lifted herself up from her crouching position over her husband and appeared to lose her seemingly doddery old woman persona. She looked Anita straight in the eye. "You're absolutely right. You do need to attend to your friend. Don't you go worrying about us. We'll be fine." As she spoke, Anita looked up towards the window of the first floor apartment where Myra's expressionless silhouette dominated the window frame. Her stillness reminded Anita of school days when their predacious secondary school head teacher would stand at her office window looking out over the playground area ready to swoop on any unsuspecting child.

Anita looked up for a few more seconds before turning to Mrs Mortnel, wishing her and her husband all the best. She then made her way towards the apartment block. Why did Mrs Mortnel feel that she needed to attend to Myra? Was she also worried about her? Had she seen signs of stress?

As Anita reached the front entrance, the ambulance finally began to make its noisy way towards the hospital. She really hoped that Mrs Mortnel's optimism for her husband was not unfounded.

The silhouette had now moved to answer the apartment door; the expression was still unclear, as was the tone of voice, "You thought that the ambulance was for me."

"I did wonder."

"Well it wasn't."

"I know that now."

"Why did you think it was for me?"

"The manuscript."

"The manuscript is pure fiction, Anita."

"You're okay?"

"I'm fine."

Although unconvinced by this robotic being that still barred the threshold to the apartment, Anita's resolve to talk things through seem to dissipate. She did not know what to say; she suddenly felt stupid and exposed. "Well if you're okay."

"As I said, I'm fine. Go and enjoy your weekend." And with that, Myra closed the door.

Anita had thought that she would be invited in, but that clearly was not going to happen. She momentarily considered hammering on the door, but she knew Myra: once she had decided on a course of action, nothing would change her mind.

If she had entered, Anita would have been appalled. The apartment was a war zone of clothes, soiled nappies, toys, all lying where they had been dropped. The dishes in the kitchen had not been washed for days and nothing resembling housework had been attempted for weeks: no dusting, no vacuuming, no cleaning.

In fact, unknown to Anita at the time, she would only ever enter the apartment on one more occasion, a fortnight later.

Another Two Weeks: Thursday

Myra was so tired. But she believed that everything was ready.

The door bell rang. She was expecting Anita. She had apologised to her on more than one occasion for her abruptness on the night of Mr Mortnel's heart attack but why was her friend over half an hour early this evening? She wanted Anita to stop worrying about her and had played the superficial 'I'm fine' card when they chatted in recent days on the mobile. However, this was much too early. Anita was always punctual; she had an uncanny knack of always being on time. Never early. Never late. This was not the occasion for her to change her habits.

Myra shuffled sluggishly towards the door to see who was there. She blinked in surprise to find Warrant Officer Mortnel on her threshold, but not his old belligerent self. This was a new man. A softer man.

"Mr Mortnel. You're back from the hospital. You're up and about. It's. . . it's. . . it's um good to see you."

"Yes, I'm feeling a little fragile but much better than I was and recovered enough to be discharged from the hospital. I found this on the floor outside your door." He held a small rag doll towards her. "I'm assuming it belongs to that lovely little girl of yours."

Myra paused momentarily. "Um. Yes it does. Thank you."

Not knowing what else to say, she turned to go back into the apartment, but this new, unrecognisable man spoke again.

"I've bought her a little gift." He put his hand into his pocket to retrieve a bag. From out of the bag he took a casket; crumpled the bag back into his pocket and looked down at the casket in the palm of his hand. He cleared his throat. "It's just a small thing. A trinket." And for the second time within a few moments, he held out his hand to her. "She may not be old enough for it yet but perhaps in years to come she might like to wear it. Do take it."

Myra took the box and slowly opened the lid. Inside was a beautiful silver chained necklace with a shining teddy bear pendant.

She was absolutely lost for words. She looked blearily into his eyes. Was this really the same man who had rapped on her door so many times to complain about the noise? Was this the man who had called her a scrounger, a parasite, a layabout, a freeloader?

"I don't know what to say."

"You don't have to say anything young lady. We both know how we have felt about each other in the past. But circumstances change and sometimes we need to look at what we have said, what we have done, and just reassess where we are." He smiled and turned away, an old man who with one small action had changed the narrative.

"Thank you."

Can a person change that drastically? Can a person undo past wrongs so easily? Was it possible?

She looked down at the chain in her hands; it was stunning. She turned the pendant over to see a small inscription. "To Miriam. With love."

The warrant officer's wife arrived. She gently slipped her arm into that of her husband and the two of them walked together towards the lift. Mrs Mortnel looked back over her shoulder and winked. "We're just popping down to the shops. Is there anything you want?"

"Oh no, thank you." Myra watched incredulously as the elderly couple, whose joy for life seemed to have been revitalised, both stepped into the lift and it travelled out of sight.

She stood there on the threshold for some time. No, not everyone can change. Not everyone was that. . . what was the word? Brave or weak? The Kilmans had changed because she had used her authorial control over them; she possessed absolute power in deciding their outcomes. But this was real life. Warrant Officer Mortnel's leopard spots were still there, albeit out of view under the surface at the moment. He had suffered a scare. Making amends would be short-lived and he would be back to his cantankerous old self soon enough. She was pretty sure that in the long term he was incapable of change. However, one thing she knew for certain was that she herself definitely could not and would not change. Her fate was predetermined.

She turned from the corridor and stepped over the threshold of her apartment. The room began to spin in front of her. She pressed her body against the door to close it and slowly slid down onto the floor. She closed her eyes and the small casket fell silently onto the carpet beside her, the silver chain remained in her hand. It was the last thing she saw before the darkness overwhelmed her.

Anita rang and rang the bell. Myra had told her to bring her door key, saying that she needed to get the lock changed as she had inadvertently lost one of her keys and feared a break-in. Anita didn't feel that she should use the key now to get into the property as to open the door unannounced would be an invasion of privacy, but 'needs must' and she dived into her handbag for it. The key turned easily but something was blocking the way. She pushed. She called. Then she saw the hand fall in the gap between the door and the wall. The obstacle was a body: Myra's body.

The Mortnels were not at home as she had seen them exiting the lift at the ground floor and they would have been the first to hear the commotion had they been there. However, Howie Redman, the council maintenance engineer, was working on the floor above. He heard the screaming and rushed down to the first floor to help.

The ambulance was called. The police were called. All futile. Myra was gone. She had taken an overdose. She had wanted, it would seem, Anita to be the one who would find her. This is why she had asked her to bring her spare key so that she could get into the apartment. Yet this was all conjecture, as there was no note. Why? Why was there no suicide note?

Having spoken to her unexpected visitor, Myra had not had the time to get further than the door before she had collapsed.

Answers?

The following evening, Anita sat at her home in pure dejection. All night she had tossed and turned with very little, if any, sleep. All day she had lurched around her bedsit in a daze, having neither the courage nor the energy to contact anyone. She needed to be alone. The local police had telephoned to check her well-being; did they think that they would soon be having another suicide on their hands? Other than that, she had not spoken to anyone.

She sat with a cold, untouched mug of coffee which had stood before her on the table for half an hour. She thought about the previous weeks, months, even years. Could she have done anything more? Was the final outcome always an inevitability? Should she have read the signs sooner? Should she have stayed with Myra on the night of Mr Mortnel's heart attack? Even if she had, she knew that Myra, being Myra, would have followed her inexorable path on her own. On her own! She had not been on her own. There was Miriam. How dare she abandon that poor child. The feelings of devastation had become feelings of anger: a roller coaster of fluctuating emotions overwhelmed her. She needed to calm down. She needed to make some attempt to understand what could have led to this awful outcome.

The previous evening, the fateful evening, played out over and over and over in her head. The evening she and Howie had found Myra slumped, lifeless against the door.

Pockets of time became muddled in her head but she remembered baby Miriam's persistent, almost mournful crying. She remembered the tall, gangly police constable. What a pompous ass. So calm, so lacking in emotion. He had a job to do; she realised he had a job to do but for God's sake. This was Myra: her best friend; her kindred soul. "I'll deal with this, ma'am. Perhaps you could find the baby and look after it."

"Her. Not it. The baby is a little girl. She's called Miriam. She's a human being!" Why was she quibbling over this? She wasn't in school now.

And where was Howie? Had he or had she gone to Miriam before the police arrived? Oh yes, she remembered now. She had been sick and had had to go to the bathroom; that's why she hadn't gone to Miriam straight away. But she still couldn't remember where Howie had gone. Yes, he had gone to Miriam. Why had he gone to Miriam? What was she to him?

There was PC Gangly again. "I'll get in touch with my colleagues. They'll be here soon to look after you. In the meantime, do you think you can cope?" Perhaps he felt that keeping her occupied away from the hallway was the best approach. Of course she could cope.

She didn't say anything. She turned away and went to find baby Miriam, who was in her cot in a frenzied state: she had clearly been crying for some time. Howie stood there, looking down into the cot, not moving. She pushed him out of the way,

162

reached down and picked up the distraught infant, comforting her as best she could. She followed the practised routine to which she had become accustomed on her many visits: changing her nappy, cuddling her, rocking her gently in her arms and whispering quietly. Miriam recognised the familiar dulcet tones and, within a few minutes, had gradually calmed down.

Howie left.

Rocking the small bundle from side to side, Anita wandered into the next room: Myra's study. It was a room which was normally barred to all visitors and Anita immediately realised why.

On the main wall in front of her was a large pin-board on which there were various pieces of paper. In the centre, printed in large red capital letters was the word LITHPORT. Underneath, in black, were the words STONEHARBOUR LANE. A port was a harbour of sorts but did 'lith' mean stone? It must do. Anita immediately thought of the word monolith, which was a single stone. Lithport, the main township in the novel represented Stoneharbour Lane – a rundown area renowned for housing single parents. An area in which Myra would probably have lived had it not been for her father's wealth. The connection was pure Myra logic.

Issuing concentrically from the word LITHPORT were numerous lengths of wool, each attached to a separate small pinboard. On each pinboard was a name, sometimes two names and in some cases a photograph; there was also a short list of adjectives under most of the names.

Anita, not surprisingly, immediately honed in onto her own photograph and recognised it as having been taken when she and Myra had visited Paignton Zoo. That had been such a lovely day. For once, Myra was not flirting with anything male below the age of thirty. They joked together about this and Myra immediately ran up to the monkey cage and started posing flirtatiously in front of a very large mammal until he became bored with the whole procedure, turned his back on them and farted! Their hysterical laughter was met by some rather bemused visitors who looked disapprovingly at these two impertinent young females. That, of course, was all before Miriam arrived on the scene and changed their lives forever.

Anita's smile was fleeting as she turned her attention back to the board in front of her. Underneath the Paignton Zoo photograph Myra had written 'Anita' in black, but accompanying the name in black was a large red question mark. The adjectives were 'resourceful', 'committed' and 'understanding'.

There was also a photograph of Myra's child. Underneath this photograph was the adjective 'wished-for', and yet, ominously, it was followed by a question mark that had been written with such force that it had ripped the paper.

Mr and Mrs Vilas and Myra as a young child were together in their photograph. Myra's mother was a stunningly attractive woman and the family likeness between mother and daughter was clearly visible. But it was Myra's eyes that truly struck Anita; the eyes of the young Myra were those of her father, not her mother, however, they seemed somehow harsher and more intense. This was something that she had never considered before. Under the photograph of Mr and Mrs Vilas were the words: DEAD BUT NOT FORGOTTEN, repeated once in red and once in black. In red was the name Silva. The adjectives were 'scheming', 'sexually active', and 'manipulative'.

There was no photograph of the Mortnels, but their names were there. Underneath Warrant Officer Mortnel's name in black was another name in red: Kilman. The adjectives were 'military', 'educated' and 'abrupt'. Underneath Mrs Mortnel's name in black was another name in red: May Kilman. The adjectives were 'oppressed' and 'loyal'.

One thread of wool was dangling lifelessly from the central section. Anita assumed that it had been attached to the pinboard where there were two separate drawing pins but no connecting thread. Underneath one of the pins there was nothing where, on the other boards there was a photograph; perhaps there had originally been a photograph on this one too. The space left between this first drawing pin and the second drawing pin seemed to match the size of the other photographs on the wall, so this was an obvious assumption. The second drawing pin doggedly clung on to a torn piece of paper on which there had been writing. Because of the tear, only some of what had been written was showing. In red at the top of the piece of paper was 'Kimberley (AKA Kim)' and underneath it the beginning of another name: Mike B. The rip had sliced the next letter which could have been an 'r' or the beginning of an 'm' or an 'n'. It was highly unlikely that the letter following a 'B' was either an 'm'; or an 'n' but it was impossible to tell. If the theory worked out in practice, the letter was also more likely to be an 'r' as there was neither an 'n' nor a second 'm' in the name 'Kimberley'.

Anita started to feel overwhelmed by it all. She felt dizzy, but needed to be aware that she was cradling a small, utterly exhausted child. She heard a sound in the hallway and just as she was turning around to leave the room, noticed a screwed up photograph in the wastepaper basket. She was unsure as to why she had looked there, perhaps it was just a habit, one that on a number of occasions had helped her find useful clandestine notes written in her classes and thrown into the waste bin on the way out at the end of the lesson by students who would never dream that their teacher might take a look. On one occasion she had even found her car keys in there.

She quickly retrieved the photograph, without anyone seeming to notice. She briefly considered secreting it into the folds of the small blanket that she had wrapped around Miriam, who could be innocently complicit: the idea seemed disingenuous. Anita just had time to stuff it into her own pocket.

"Are you alright, ma'am? You shouldn't be in here."

"Yes. Sorry. Miriam is happier when I walk about with her in my arms and I got a bit fed up of just wandering around her bedroom so I came in here." She brushed her hands over the papers that were scattered around the computer which sat in front of the pinboarded wall: scribbles, notes, crossings-out.

"Try not to touch anything, ma'am. We need to look through all of this. My colleague here will relieve you of the babe in arms until we can contact any of her close relatives."

They turned to leave the room but not before Anita took one last look at the eyes of Mr Silva and his daughter.

In the corridor Anita was approached by a female police constable. "My name is W.P.C Hill and you are. . ?" The uniform suited her and somehow she managed to achieve a look of businesslike efficiency tinged with concern and empathy.

"Mann. Miss Mann." Anita also stayed with the use of surnames. This was clearly not a friendly chat and as sympathetic as the woman standing in front of her might be, the formalities remained in place.

"We need to find close members of this young lady's family. Perhaps the child's father." She held her arms out to take Miriam from Anita's arms.

"Arthur. Arthur Vilas."

The woman paused and in an undisguised tone of surprise responded. "The Arthur Vilas of Vilas Enterprises?"

"Yes."

"He's the father of this baby?"

Anita suddenly realised her mistake. "Oh no. He's. . . he's Myra's father."

"Myra being the young lady whom you found in the corridor."

"Yes."

"Well, that's a start. And what about the baby's father?"

"I don't know. None of us know. Myra would never say. She told me that she didn't need to have anything to do with the father and we didn't need to know who he was."

"We?"

"Oh me and anyone else that she was acquainted with." She wasn't going to inadvertently mention Arthur Vilas again; she had already made that mistake once. "She said that she didn't need any financial help from the father or. . . or. . . support. It wasn't that he had done anything wrong. She just didn't want any help. Apparently he was happy with that. She wasn't in a long term relationship with him. Myra was. . . well I suppose you would describe her as being quite independent."

"So she didn't want any support at all?"

"Yes, that's right."

Anita continued to give the policewoman any details that she needed and later on she was driven home. The police were not happy about her driving that evening despite her assurances to the contrary, insisting that she was perfectly all right. In the end she conceded to their wishes and agreed to be taken home and to collect her car the next day.

With the anger gone, the dejection returned. She mulled over her mistake with the police woman. Why did she blurt out Myra's father's name when the woman had asked about Miriam's father? Why did she say 'Arthur' rather than 'Mr Vilas', and why on earth did she say his name at all? Of course he wasn't Miriam's father; he couldn't be. However, Myra had managed to sow those seeds of doubt in her manuscript.

She started to think about the possible identity of Miriam's father. Would it help to find him? Why didn't Myra want her to know who it was? The implications of the manuscript played devilishly on her mind. No, it couldn't be Arthur Vilas; that was unthinkable. She had to find the true father.

Myra, it had to be said, was a flirt. There was the young chap at the sports club. There was the teacher at her school. . . but surely that was only a one-off after Miriam was born? And why had Howie stood mesmerised over Miriam's cot? Then there was the photograph.

She leaned across and picked up the crumpled image from the coffee table. Was this a picture of the father?

She tried to press out the creases with the palm of her hand for a better view. She looked closely. She recognised this man. She had definitely seen him before, but where?

She sat back and placed the photograph on her lap. A car engine revved outside. Of course, that was it. She looked at the photograph again. It was the man who had fixed her car.

Mike B. . .

Having collected her car from outside Myra's apartment, Anita drove it to the garage. She parked a block away from the Delabole Garage and walked there at a leisurely pace. Despite her burning desire to get this whole business clear in her mind, she had to give herself time to think things through and decide how best to broach the subject with a man she had only met a couple of times and even then, only in connection with fixing her car. She had not really been concerned about his personality or how he conducted his social life away from the garage; they were not important at the time. Perhaps she now needed to view him from a different perspective.

When she arrived, she hesitated. Her body language must have been such that she caught the attention of a garage worker there, an older man who soon realised that she was looking for some assistance.

"Can I help?"

"Uh, yes I recently had my car fixed by one of your mechanics. I think his name was Mike. I wonder if he's about."

"Oh yes. I'll get him." He didn't actually 'get him' as such but just turned his head and shouted, "Mike! Lady to see you." Anita wasn't sure that even this man's mighty roar could be heard above the raucous dissonant sounds of Radio One emanating from the workshop. He turned towards Anita, "Do you mind if I ask your name?"

"No, that's fine. It's Anita Mann."

"Well, he won't be long, Miss Mann."

Interesting that he should make the assumption of singleness.

Mike had obviously heard his name called, accustomed to the volume of the radio presumably, as it was seconds later that he walked out in his mechanic's overalls. He was wiping his greasy hands on a cloth that looked even greasier, but perhaps it was just a token gesture to show the customer some degree of cleanliness. She hoped he wouldn't want to exchange handshakes. There was no doubt that he was the man from the photograph: good looking in a rugged sort of way, with close cropped hair, just starting to recede at the temples.

"Yes? Any problem?"

She didn't know where to start. She had had most of the morning to think about this but when it came to it she really didn't know what to say and just blurted out, "I'm a close friend of Myra Vilas."

The transformation was immediate: his face suddenly became deeply wary and the tone of voice changed from one of polite enquiry to one of deep suspicion. He paused, "Right, and has she sent you for some reason?"

Of course! He wasn't aware that Myra was dead; why should he be with her death having been only days before? She started stammering in a pathetic apologetic way, "Oh no. It's just that. It's just that." She took a deep breath; her eyes started to well up with tears. "She's dead."

What was she thinking? To suddenly broadcast this unwelcome sound-bite. How must this man feel to be unexpectedly faced with such devastating news totally out of the blue? "Oh I've gone about this in all the wrong way. I've just got this all wrong. I'm sorry, it's just that I found your photograph in amongst her things and I recognised you from having done my car. I didn't realise that you had known her. And well, her baby Miriam, she. . ."

A hand was held up. "Stop. This sounds like it's going to be a long conversation and. . . " he indicated the garage, smiled apologetically and continued, "I am supposed to be working."

"I'm sorry."

"I tell you what. As it's a Saturday, I finish early. I should be done here by just before three. My girlfriend works all day every alternate Saturday and today is one of those days: lucky girl! So how about I meet you for a cup of tea at Fred's Cafe just down the road there. Okay?"

She nodded. And all she could think was, 'So there's a girlfriend and he has made this fact very clear.' Anita wasn't sure if he would meet up with her but she was prepared to think he would; for some reason she already trusted, even liked, this man whom she had only met fleetingly before in the role of a workman fixing her car. "Yes, that's fine."

Under normal circumstances, Anita would have used the next couple of free hours productively to mark some books, contact a friend, do some shopping. But these were not normal circumstances and she knew that her state of mind would not allow her to achieve anything constructive. She just wandered. She wandered to her car, past her car and on towards the canal. She was not heading anywhere in particular but submissively following where her feet led.

The next two hours were a blur. She walked aimlessly along the canal path; there were no decisions to make as to whether to turn left or right so she merely carried on. A small family of swans sedately glided towards her in the hope of a few breadcrumbs but soon became disinterested when they realised she had nothing for them. A group of friends, probably from the nearby college, passed by in canoes, laughing at the lack of control as one of their members struggled to keep a straight line and almost collided with the canal edge. Their voices bounced around the sides of the bridge beneath which they paddled. When Anita reached the bridge herself, drops of water fell from above onto her head and down the back of her neck as she walked beneath.

A little further on she had to lean against the moss covered wall on hearing the warning 'brrring' of a cyclist's bell as he approached from behind. These small everyday yet significant events that would usually register in her head for future

h

descriptive work with the students meant little to her today and it was not until she reached the end of the walkway that she even thought about looking at her watch. It was time to make her way to Fred's Cafe.

As Anita entered the cafe, the tinkle of the bell above the door made her feel exposed; although not very loud, it was a sudden sound that she had not really expected. If she had had the sense to look above the door before she entered, she would have seen the traditional brass wall mounted bell dangling in such a way as to just be caught by the door as it opened. But she hadn't looked up; she had looked straight ahead in the hope that this would give her the courage not to turn back.

She felt like a stranger might do when inadvertently entering a secret poker game taking place in the darkened room behind a snooker club. But this was a cafe, pure and simple: it was open to the public and there were no small groups of men huddling around tables squinting at their cards in a gloomy, smoke-filled atmosphere. Quite the opposite, in fact, as the cafe was very light and airy. Nobody looked her way: there were no suspicious glances as a Royal Flush was held closely to the chest while the Full House was smugly placed on the table. In fact, the group of four white shirted, grey suited men in the corner just carried on with what she surmised as being business talk; the two elderly ladies seated to her left by the window were chatting and giggling over some conspiratorial snippet of gossip; and the man at the other window sat, totally focused on reading his newspaper.

Fred's Cafe was not what she had pictured it to be. For some reason, probably merely because of its close proximity to the garage and, it has to be said, some rather rundown small shops hanging onto their businesses by a tiny pecuniary thread whilst others had been forced to close, she had imagined somewhere a little less salubrious. She had envisioned a roadside drinking hole for lorry drivers and tired travellers with a large man, dressed in a grimy once-white apron covered in greasy smirches, behind the bar flipping beef-burgers, unconcerned as the fat below sizzled angrily in front of him. Possibly it was the name that had also influenced her expectations, but Fred's Cafe turned out to be a

170

very welcoming, modern establishment with wooden chairs and benches, designer cushions dotted about, and a huge blackboard stretching across the length of one of the side walls and covered with beautiful cursive writing enticing the customer to spend money on a variety of Fred's Specials.

Anita selected a small table, by the wall to the right. A central table didn't seem suitable for the occasion; it had the potential to become too much a focus of attention. There were no booths but by choosing a side table it would mean that she, or hopefully they, would not be in anyone's direct line of vision. When she sat down, she started to feel anxious that he wouldn't come and if he did come, what was she going to say? What exactly did she want to achieve? Why hadn't she given these things any thought during the past two hours?

It was gone three, the allocated time, but she was prepared to wait a bit longer; she would feel stupid walking back out again. Before she had had a chance to order anything, the distinctive tinkle of the bell above the cafe door sounded.

Mike walked straight over to her, "I'm sorry I'm late. I had a few minor issues to sort out. Tea?"

She nodded.

He called over to the lady at the counter. "Two teas please, Mrs H."

"Right you are, Mike. Two secs."

Mike lifted his chair back. Just a small point but Anita was impressed. He hadn't scraped the chair thoughtlessly along the floor like most of her students would have done and did every day despite being asked not to do so.

She immediately liked this man.

She hadn't realised just how tall he was. He must have been about six feet three or four. He had abandoned his overalls for a white tee shirt under which there was undoubtedly a body that had clearly benefited from regular workouts in the gym. He was all muscle. Big chest, small waste; just like an hourglass. She had to bite her lip to stop herself smiling as images of Mr Incredible from the Pixar film 'The Incredibles' sprung to mind.

He was the first to speak and broached the poignant topic immediately, but it was baby Miriam that was his main concern, not Myra. "Is the baby okay?" In the cold light of day, this was a logical priority but Anita was mildly surprised.

171

"Yes, Miriam is absolutely fine. She's with Myra's father. He'll look after her."

"Well, I hope he'll be more loving than she was." The 'she' to whom he referred was clearly Myra, but there wasn't any bitterness in this comment. It was stated as a definitive matter of fact.

Mrs H brought the teas. "Anything else?"

Mike looked at Anita enquiringly and she shook her head. "No, that's fine Mrs H. We'll give you a shout if we need anything more." He turned back to Anita, "So, what happened?"

Anita took a deep breath and began her explanation. "It appears that she committed suicide. A drug overdose. I was the one who found her. Last Thursday evening. She had invited me over even though it was a weekday evening and I had school the next day. I don't know if you recall me saying I'm a teacher? I rarely go out on weekday evenings – marking, lesson preparation, all that sort of thing.

"Anyway, I really wanted to see her as I had been getting pretty worried about her state of mind recently. I saw this invitation as a good reason to ensure she was okay. She clearly wasn't. I don't know if she deliberately did this or if she didn't realise the strength of the pills. I just wouldn't have thought she was the type. Perhaps I was wrong." Anita looked down and nervously rubbed her hands together.

"Why had you been getting worried about her state of mind?" This small prompt was all that was necessary for her to continue.

"There were little things that were just so out of character. She had got rid of her cleaner and had let the flat get dirty. She had also let herself go. By her high standards, anyway. Things that other people might not notice. But I did. She had stopped wearing make-up. She still went out when there was a small ladder in her tights. She wouldn't have done this before. She wouldn't even have gone down to the local corner shop if she had noticed a ladder in her tights. And then there was the manuscript."

"Manuscript?"

"She wrote a manuscript and it was a sort of parallel with her life, but set in a different era. She gave me a copy of it to read and it took me a long time to realise, too long actually, but one of the characters attempted suicide but only when one of the other characters was there to save her. It was as if Myra intended to do

172

the same yet she wanted me to realise that she wanted to be saved and I was the one who had to save her. It was a cry for help, I suppose, and the only way she could let me know was through her writing. She was never someone who seemed able to talk things through; it was almost as if we all had to read her mind. Her public persona was always one of self-control."

Mike frowned, "Yes, I know that one."

"It's really difficult to explain but all the characters in the manuscript had a parallel partner, for want of a better description, in real life; you were one of the characters, but female.

"In her study at the apartment, pinned up on the wall above her computer, were the names of the characters in her manuscript and by each of them was the name of someone whom she knew in real life. Each character's name was an anagram of a person whom she knew. The paper with your equivalent character just said Kim (AKA Kimberley), but it was ripped. Underneath was the name Mike B; the rest had been torn away. But I found a crumpled photograph in the wastepaper bin next to her computer and recognised the photograph of you from when you fixed my car and I remembered that your name was Mike."

He smiled, "I'm impressed." He paused, clearly thinking about what she had just said, and then continued in a more matter-of-fact tone, "My name is Mike Bryle; an anagram of the name Kimberley, I believe."

This time it was Anita's turn to pause. She swallowed hard and decided to dip her toe in the water, or perhaps dive in completely, "I wondered if you were, are, Miriam's father."

His head tipped back and he looked briefly up to the ceiling before returning to look her straight in the eyes, "Is that what the manuscript implied? Yes, I suppose it would. I did go out with Myra. She was beautiful, I really thought my luck was in: a lowly car mechanic, nothing special, going out with an author, and an author from a rich family. I know I work out and some might say I'm good looking but to many that's all: a practical guy with not much for brains. I thought that perhaps Myra saw beyond that. I actually did well in my GCSEs at school, but made the decision not to carry on with A Levels. I didn't really see the point. I didn't want to go on to university. I'd always loved cars so that's the route I took. I'm not too sure that either my parents or indeed my teachers were very happy about it but I was pretty determined. If

I wanted to study again at a later date, I could do that on my own terms. There are plenty of evening schools about.

"Anyway I met Myra and as I said a moment ago, she was beautiful and for once seemed to be someone who appreciated me, who saw the real me." He sighed. "But, you know, in hindsight I think she just used me. We went out for a while, had a good time, but she just seemed selfish: everything had to be her way. She didn't want to meet my parents; she was always on about how her father let her down and how he was responsible for her mother's death. She openly flirted with other men right in front of me. I don't know if she wanted to make me jealous to see how I would react but I'm not a jealous kind of guy and I'm certainly not aggressive."

He took a sip of his tea. "Then later, quite a bit later, she informed me she was pregnant. We had a bit of a row as she had told me she was on the pill and that we were safe. I certainly wasn't ready to be a father but if I was then I would have helped out and not only financially. I would have looked after any child of mine. I love children. But Miriam was definitely not my child. Definitely."

He saw the puzzled look on Anita's face.

"She had at least one affair while she was going out with me. Yes, she had all the dates and everything that to all intents and purposes seemed to indicate that I was the dad but I wasn't."

"How do you know? How are you so sure?"

"As soon as I discovered that she had been seeing other men while I was going out with her, I finished the relationship. I believe in loyalty; I believe in being faithful. But when she came to me one day, telling me that she was pregnant and she wanted me back and she had been a fool to act in the way she did, it spooked me. I wanted to be sure, absolutely sure. I don't have sexual problems as such but it turns out that I'm impotent. It's something to do with sperm production or sperm transport. I'm sure you don't need the details.

"I felt really embarrassed at first. You know, stupid as it sounds, a man's masculinity is connected to his ability to have children. I felt humiliated, emasculated I suppose. I didn't want to be the butt of my mates' jokes: 'shooting blanks' and all that.

"Well, when I met my present girlfriend soon after, I knew she was the one for me so I've been entirely open with her. We both want children in the future. She's really supportive and I'm seeing a doctor; she goes along with me when she can. So you see, I'm not Miriam's father."

He put his hands on to his thighs and leaned back; the corners of his mouth formed into a smile. "Actually, I find it mildly amusing that my equivalent in this manuscript of Myra's is a female; she wouldn't have been able to have children with whoever Myra is in the manuscript, either."

Anita expected a hiatus at this point, yet there wasn't. He continued, but there was a greater seriousness in his tone.

"She was not a good mother, you know that don't you. Whenever I saw her with the baby she was on the mobile phone or she was talking to someone in the street; always ignoring the little girl. I saw them fairly recently in the park, Myra was sitting on one of the benches; she could have taken the child out of the pushchair, but she didn't. She just sat there looking out to space. I don't know if she had some sort of post natal depression or something like that but she should have seen someone. Perhaps I sound selfish but that child wasn't mine; she wasn't my responsibility."

Anita had sat and listened to his every word. She not only believed him but knew that, deep down inside, she agreed with him. Myra was not a good mother.

She sipped her now cold tea.

"Miss Mann."

"Oh please call me Anita."

"Anita. This might sound a bit airy-fairy, but I was merely one chapter in Myra's life. She turned the page and I was forgotten. You, you were a good friend. In fact, come to think of it, she mentioned you many times when we were together. You feel a greater sense of responsibility than I do. The book is still open for you but take my advice: don't dwell there too long, it's Myra's book not yours. You need to be the protagonist in your own text, in your own future. Myra no longer has a future; you do."

With that he got up and this time he did stretch out his hand, "It's been good meeting with you and I'm sorry that I haven't been able to be of more help, but if you ever need your car fixing again, you know where I am." He turned and left to the tinkling of a small brass door bell.

"Another cup?"

"Oh, no thank you."

175

"He's a nice lad that Mike, isn't he?"

"Yes, he is. How much do I owe you?"

Mrs H gave a short laugh. "Nothing dear. He came in at lunchtime and paid up front. That's the sort of lad he is."

He was also the sort of lad who would not have been persuaded, even by Myra, to abandon his own child. He was not Miriam's father; Anita was sure of that. If she wanted to find Miriam's father, she had to look elsewhere.

The Sports Club

Anita was familiar with the local sports club that Myra had frequented when she was on a 'fitness fad': a brief sojourn of about two months at the most as far as Anita could recall. However, it was certainly long enough for Myra to get to know the staff and possibly even some of the regular fitness enthusiasts. But, apropos Anita's opinion for what is was worth, it was yet another of Myra's short lived whims which gave her the opportunity to purchase all the expensive latest fashions in sports gear which were worn on only one or two occasions, folded up and then put into a cupboard. There was no sense of the unexpected when the impulse to keep fit came to its inevitable end, but she was also not in the least surprised that her flirtatious friend had been seeing one of the fitness instructors for fitness of a different nature. It had not taken her very long to get to know yet another man more intimately then was necessary, and the fact that it was one of the instructors now narrowed the field down a bit as to the possible identity of Miriam's father.

Anita parked her aging vehicle in the sports club car park, yet stayed there unmoving, wondering whether this quest she had set herself was worthwhile and in anyone's best interests. She had deliberately parked where she could sit and watch the people coming and going: it was the staff members in particular on whom she focused with their distinctive track suits emblazoned across the back with the sports club slogan. She watched from the semi-comfort of her driver's seat, gradually becoming less and less enthusiastic about her self-appointed task as she started to acknowledge its enormity and its possible futility.

It would not do any harm just to go in and perhaps make a few enquiries. She could pretend to be a prospective member, pick up a leaflet about opening times, look at the facilities whilst surreptitiously watching out for male members of staff who could have been Myra's 'type'.

She slammed her hand down in frustration onto the steering wheel. What was the point? What was she trying to prove?

She started up the engine and drove off, out of the car park and back home.

The Funeral: The Final Act

Anita sat towards the back of the church; the hard wooden pew afforded no alleviation from the discomfort she felt, both physically and emotionally. There were about thirty people dressed in various colours as if attending a wedding, not a funeral: it all seemed so incongruous but Myra had apparently insisted that no one wore black. One man, sitting in the front row defied this directive, his touch of rebellion made all the more noticeable due to the distinctive black gabardine and his tall stature. She wondered if he would give a tribute during the service, and if so, what he would say. It had also been his decision to hold the funeral in church; Myra had not wanted this either.

Anita did not recognise everyone in the congregation but she did not expect to; there were, however, a few familiar faces. Mike Bryle was there fiddling uncomfortably with his tie that restricted his thick muscular neck. Beside him sat a diminutive and pretty young woman: presumably his present girlfriend. Howie Redman was there, doubtless representing the council, although she still suspected that he had fallen for Myra's allure at some stage. There was no sports club representative as far as she could tell. She felt somehow gratified that the Mortnels had made it. Mr Mortnel, Warrant Officer Class 1, was looking resplendent in his service uniform. He coughed rather loudly and his wife, placing her hand on his lap, looked sympathetically and lovingly toward him. A brief sip from a small plastic bottle of water was all that was needed. Anita was pleased that he seemed to be recovering well. She also vaguely recognised one or two faces from secondary school, but she knew that Myra had not really kept in close contact with anyone other than herself.

Just in front of her a young boy of about ten, presumably dressed in his Sunday best, delighted in picking his nose and then looking closely at the contents before his enjoyment was abruptly halted by a swift cuff to the ear. This was immediately followed by a stage whispered, "Cut that out. You're in church." Anita smiled. He would probably be one of her pupils in a year or two.

Most of the congregation comprised of young people who at some time or other had been touched by Myra's charm. The smile soon dissipated and Anita found it impossible to dislodge the lump in her throat as she looked down at the service sheet:

A Service of Thanksgiving for the life of
Marilyn Donna Vilas
3rd April 1993 - 27th May 2018

And all these years she had believed her friend's name to be Myra, simply Myra. But, of course, there was never anything simple about her. Even at school her registered name was definitely Myra. Another secret she had managed to skilfully conceal. Oh, how she missed her.

Below these printed words was the photograph of a beautiful teenager, taken during the carefree summer of 2008 when all the troubles of the world were far away. Anita opened the folded sheet in order to follow the order of the service. It was time for the Reverend Graham Staunton to give a few welcoming words before introducing the opening hymn, 'The Day Thou Gavest Lord Has Ended'. His tribute followed, saying how all who knew her should remember the joyful, cheeky yet independent young lady that was Marilyn Donna Vilas. He gave a few anecdotes that had clearly been passed on to him by her father and then a second hymn, 'I Vow To Thee My Country' was sung. She doubted very much that either of these hymns had been chosen by the now deceased woman whom she was proud to call a friend. No other personal tributes were given. Perhaps the Blessing was intended to be the ultimate act to touch the hearts of those present but it was Myra's final touch that left a lasting indelible mark: the recessional music was 'The Best' by Tina Turner.

Myra loved to sing that song at full volume but she always sang, "I'm the best, better than all the rest" instead of, "You're the best, better than all the rest". That was Myra.

The coffin was carried out to the graveyard for the final act: Myra's interment. People stood around afterwards talking for a while and then made their way home. It had been decided that there would not be a wake.

All the mourners returned to their cars and had driven away to their separate destinations and their separate lives. Two elderly men stood by, ready to fill in the recently dug hole and cover the young mother forever. The tall gentleman, dressed in a black gabardine mackintosh following the contours of his body down to his calves, picked his way slowly over the sodden ground towards the newly dug grave; the rain had stopped for the moment at least. In his right hand he carried a large folded black umbrella; his left hand was deeply planted into the pocket of his coat. He asked the two men if they could afford him a moment or two by the graveside and they willingly obliged, walking away to have an unexpected and welcome smoke.

He stood looking down upon the coffin with its handfuls of earth that had been thrown down, and, draped sadly on one particular clump of earth towards the upper end of the coffin, lay a single red rose. His gaze was then taken by a small bouquet at his feet with its attached note, "Mummy. I will always love you. Miriam xxx." A gesture perhaps from the unknown father or possibly a touch of thoughtfulness from Anita. A small teddy bear lay forlornly by the side staring out at the world with sad, pebble eyes; around its neck was a small label, 'With love now and always. Anita xxx.' No tears would fall from that stoic, furry little creature; the tears that fell came from the man's eyes. He made no attempt to wipe them away.

He then became aware of someone standing behind him; he turned and came face to face with a young woman. She fell into his arms and the body wrenching sobs racked her whole being. "I should have saved her. It was there; written in her own words; a cry for help and I was the one who was supposed to help her."

He carefully drew her away from him, held her shoulders at arms' length and looked uncomprehendingly into her eyes. "What are you talking about? There was nothing that you could do."

"But I was Tania. Don't you see? Tania saved Silva's daughter. All the names were anagrams of real people: real people in Myra's life. Parallel lives. Tania is an anagram of Anita and Tania saved the life of Mary. And Mary is an anagram of Myra. Even

179

Tania's surname is a man's name and what's my surname? Don't you see; it was a call for help." She paused. "You didn't read the manuscript, did you? You wouldn't understand."

Arthur Silva took Anita's hand and guided her towards a nearby wooden bench, where they both sat down.

"I did read the manuscript, after you left a second copy of it with me. I couldn't sleep that night and I read it all. Word for word."

"Then you'll know that I'm right."

"No, Anita. Not entirely. Yes, the names were anagrams and they each represented someone in Myra's life, but you weren't Tania. Nobody could ever be Tania; she was perfect and pure, untainted by the world in which she found herself. No one could ever aspire to that. Tania was, in more ways than one, a work of fiction and nothing more. If you were anybody, you were Lisa."

"Lisa?" This was totally inconceivable.

"Yes. Calm, organised Lisa."

Myra's words at the time of the boys' fight came back to her, "You're always calm in a crisis, Anita."

Arthur Vilas continued, "You said yourself that your parents didn't give any of your siblings a second name. Only you. Your father with his slightly distorted sense of humour wanted to call you Isla as a joke but your mother persuaded him to call you Anita yet, against her better judgement it would seem, reluctantly agreed to letting him call you Isla as a second name. What harm could it do? No one uses people's second names; it was your family's private joke. Isla Mann." He stopped for a moment, drew breath and continued. "You do realise that Myra knew about our affair. I don't know how, but she obviously found out about the two of us."

Anita was speechless.

"Oh, I don't suppose she wanted you to try to kill me, like Lisa killed Silva, but she certainly wanted to ruin me. She wanted to put a rift between the two of us."

Anita began to consider what was being said. She formulated the ideas and thoughts that flooded her mind and started to verbalise these to make sense of them. "Lisa deliberately had an affair with Silva to gain information. Don't get me wrong, I think she was genuinely taken by his charm and good looks but deep down inside, she knew that he was underhand and furtive. She

180

knew that the relationship was doomed from the beginning. She was doing her job and wanted promotion. She wanted control. Is that me? Is that us? Did Myra truly believe that I was ambitious to the point of taking undue advantage in the same way?"

Arthur Vilas looked down towards the ground but said nothing. Perhaps he was not prepared to face that topic of conversation just yet, so Anita risked a new course. "Who is Miriam's father?"

The response was abrupt and immediate. "Not me! Myra had many boyfriends; it could have been any one of them. I didn't want to know. She and I argued about it on a number of occasions. But I certainly didn't rape my own daughter; that little gem of an idea was all hers.

"Anita, you and I have always avoided this conversation but perhaps it's time for us to think about it. Myra always blamed me for her mother's accident. Her mother and I argued a lot, I openly admit that. We thought about separating for a while, but we loved each other. We couldn't live without each other. It was after one of our arguments that she went for a drive and she insisted on taking Myra with her; perhaps she felt that our daughter was not safe with me. She was clearly angry and not concentrating fully on her driving. She came out in front of another car and there was nothing that the driver could do about it. He went straight into the side of the vehicle and Celia. . . Myra's mother. . . my wife, was killed instantly. Myra survived with minor bruises. In later years, she even came up with the theory that I had hired a killer, but it was all in her imagination. Her very vivid imagination.

"Myra was determined to live her own life. She said I was domineering and authoritarian and she wanted her own daughter to have nothing to do with me. I had ruined her life and she was not going to let me ruin the life of her daughter. She accused me of manipulating her mother and being a draconian husband. Perhaps I was harsh, but I was never cruel; I would never have wished harm on either my wife or my daughter. As you know, I gave her money to buy the apartment and in the end she agreed to take it as a loan. She said that it would be paid back in full as soon as she became a successful writer. It was important to give little Miriam a good start in life. I said that it was a gift but she wanted nothing from me at all. However, it was not the only time she accepted money from me; money which I was prepared to give. She still insisted on wanting to be totally independent. She wouldn't even let me visit my own grandchild."

"But she told me you wouldn't visit her, 'He won't even come to see his own flesh and blood'. She said that you had disowned her."

"That's just not true."

"What happens now?"

"The irony is that I am the one who will look after Miriam. I have another chance, Anita, and I know that I have learned so much. Yes, perhaps I was an over-zealously strict father. I just wanted Myra to have a good education. I wanted her to be perfect. . . like Tania, I suppose. But what is perfection? I hope that I have mellowed. In fact, I know that I have mellowed; you have helped me to do that. I hope that I am more understanding now. As for you and me. . . that is your decision. I have grown to love you. I know that I have deliberately kept my family affairs from you; I didn't want to damage your deep friendship with Myra in any way. But as far as you and I are concerned, the age gap means nothing to me. I admit that at first, when I found out who you were and how close you were to Myra, I saw it as a way to at least hear about her and my grandchild. But as time went on, I. . . " His hand slowly slipped out of its clasp with Anita's hand.

She looked at him, "You need time. . . and so do I. You need to be with your granddaughter and then who knows?"

Arthur Vilas reached into his pocket and took out an envelope. "There's a letter here to you from Myra. It arrived at my house the day she died. It was inside a card that she sent to me. I haven't opened the letter; I don't know what it says."

"What did the card say?"

"It had a photograph stuck on the front of my wife and myself, but there was a rip down the centre between the two of us with Myra's name printed vertically in the gap. Inside she had written the words; 'To my dearest father. With my deepest regrets. I am truly sorry for all I have done and I take full responsibility. Please forgive me. Your ever loving Myra.'

"Anita, I really do not know if there is any further explanation in the letter she has written to you, but whatever she may or may not have done it would not make me love her any less. There are imperfections in all of us and the first step towards loving others is to admit to and recognise those imperfections in ourselves so that we are then able to forgive them in others."

Anita took the envelope from his hand. She slowly rose, lent down and kissed him on the forehead, then walked away. When she reached her car at the edge of the walled graveyard she turned back to where she saw a very lonely figure, sitting forlornly on a wooden bench. An isolated figure with no one to turn to. But perhaps, just perhaps, he would love and cherish the 'wished for child' and one day that child would love and cherish him in return. As for his future with a young teacher of English, only time would tell.

She drove home, made herself a coffee and sat down to read the letter from Myra.

The Letter: Final Revelations

Dearest Anita,

This has every possibility of sounding like the worst cliché ever, but if you are reading this, I will no longer be with you. The likelihood is that I will have deliberately taken my life: an act that I have seriously considered for a very long time. Longer than you can imagine.

You might be wondering at this point why I decided to embark upon a new manuscript when I have harboured unwavering and long-term suicidal thoughts. The answer is simple: I wanted some semblance of control over my remaining life, however brief that may or may not turn out to be. As you are undoubtedly aware, I am a bit of a control freak. After Miriam's birth, I lost this control.

I don't think I ever perceived the writing of the manuscript as being the mechanism that would stop me from ending my life but I believed it would certainly help me feel some degree of normality. My old self, if you like. Consequently, my deliberate act of defiance against my earthly existence would be committed when my thoughts were unencumbered by my seemingly insurmountable personal problems.

Don't think for one moment that I would ever commit suicide in a moment of despair. Despair is an emotion that distorts judgement. So, being in the embrace of that emotion is not the best time to call it quits.

When I first started to write my manuscript, I wanted to delve into the world of science fiction or at least a vision of our society in the future: a genre that I had not really attempted before. I initially hoped to look at the future in a positive way. I envisaged a society unencumbered by the prejudices that are the root causes of our problems in today's world. I wanted, for example, to see a future where women had parity with men. But, as you know, this is not exactly how it turned out.

From the outset, the community I created had so many problems; it was dystopian in the extreme. My solution was to introduce a strong, independent young girl who could and would overcome adversity within a male dominated society. I desperately wanted to create real characters: essentially female, but characters who could also make a difference. As you know, or should do by now, I don't have a particularly high opinion of the male sector of our species.

Every day I looked out of my study window and I would see this little girl. She fascinated me and I wanted her to be my main character. She seemed so happy and self-assured despite the fact that she clearly came from a family that had very little money. And there, of course, was yet another fatal flaw in my inherited approach to life: money can solve all problems!

I saw her almost every day and whenever she met with some incident, she would cope with it in such a controlled manner. She made sensible, unselfish choices that I would never have been able to make at that age, nor since that age, if I am perfectly honest. Her love emanated out towards others; any love I possessed turned inwards towards myself and always has done. She was generous; I was, and still am, mean and selfish. It has taken a long time but I am able to admit that now, if only in writing. Some people may even feel that the act of suicide is a selfish act, but it isn't. It is the one and only truly unselfish act that I have ever undertaken.

Suicide certainly leaves a wake of devastation for those who are impacted by the death of a loved one or a friend. And, to be perfectly honest, I might already have killed myself long ago were it not for all the great experiences I've had with the one person I love. And that person is you, my dearest Anita. You. Not Miriam. Not some male hunk of a man. You.

I knew, though, the day would come when that was just not enough anymore. You could never reciprocate and love me in the same way that I loved you. And, to be honest, I have grown so very tired. Life has become less and less worth living. Some days I have hoped that a natural illness would just finish me off so that nobody would have to live with the guilt of my suicide; oh I do realise that the feeling of guilt can exist on both sides. I have certainly thought a lot about how to minimise the pain you will undoubtedly feel when you think about whether you could have done anything to stop me.

Some people believe that a person can recover from suicidal thoughts brought on by depression and despair. Apparently, or so I have been informed, you only have to find the right treatment. Social Services clearly seemed to perceive this to be the case. Those people want to prevent you from killing yourself when they feel there is some hope. You hear platitudes like 'it's only temporary' and 'you'll get better'. The reality, Anita, is that not all depression is temporary or treatable.

I certainly didn't expect help from anybody in allowing me to take my own life. Anyway, I didn't need any help; it's not that difficult to kill yourself if you want to. And that's the thing, once you realise that: you don't need anyone. You can take your life without any help no matter what anyone else thinks.

Well, let's get back to my manuscript. An indication of a good piece of fiction is when the reader can meet a character and get to know that character as a person. I truly believe that once a writer creates a convincing character, everything else falls into place. I hoped my reader would meet this young girl and get to know her but

185

I struggled to make her a convincing character because she was so perfect. She became a stereotype. I soon realised that she was the person my father wanted me to be: unreal and unachievable. Oh, I kept her in the manuscript in the hope that the little girl I saw every day outside my apartment could, in reality, change the world. But she couldn't; she was as vulnerable as every other child on earth. In fact, one day she totally disappeared and I never saw her again.

As my writing progressed, I realised that all the people within the manuscript were familiar to me; they were real people; they were the people who had shaped and were shaping my life here. As time followed its inevitable path, I couldn't tell the difference between the novel I was creating and the people in my day-to-day existence.

I am sure that you realised the parallels between the characters in my manuscript and the people in my life. Authors should never base their characters on people they know; it can cause so many problems, but I just could not help it. This manuscript was about me and my journey; it was real.

I am sure you soon became aware that every character symbolised a person within my life. But there still needed to be choice for anyone following my thought processes: anyone reading what I had written. Despite the strong indications as to who each person represented, there was still an element of choice for the reader. The anagrams may have made that choice easier, but is it always expedient to take the easy path? As you rightly said to me, I do tend to have the habit of using a smoke-screen in my writing.

In life, we have many choices; I seem to have spent a lifetime making the wrong ones. Have you realised yet whom I chose to be in life and in the manuscript? Not Mary, even though, as I am sure you realised, my name is an anagram of hers. Oh no. This was a veritable smoke-screen.

I was Silva: the man, who like me, 'was accustomed to having his own way'; the man who 'did not possess the kind of nature that could cope with adversity.' Doesn't that just sum me up?

Raymond N. A. Silva. Look at the first four letters of his name; surprise, surprise - another anagram. Mary was too minor a part for me to play. And, of course, she survived: I never intended to survive, Anita. Did you think I was Mary and my dysfunctional relationship with my father took me to the brink of self-destruction? Surely you must have realised that I am far too egotistic to take on such a minor role. And has my father ever told you my second name? It's Donna.

Like that of Silva, my self-destruction had to be complete and irreversible. He needed a helping hand to guide him towards the inevitable journey to death; I have the strength to fulfil this final act myself.

Silva hated his daughter and wanted to kill her; believe me, Anita, I have been very, very close on many an occasion. Does this fill you with horror? How easy it would have been to hold a cushion over the face of that defenceless child. I have never loved Miriam. I didn't want her. She was the archetypal mistake and, to quote the words of Samuel Beckett, 'My mistakes are my life'. I hoped that I could love her, but it wasn't to be.

Apparently, according to my doctor, I have suffered from acute postnatal depression.

Postnatal depression can affect women in many different ways. I have, as you know, always been highly confident, able to cope with anything life has thrown at me. I didn't want to confide in anyone and I certainly didn't want to feel judged for not being able to cope. I suppose nobody would ever have described me as being a happy person, but since Miriam's birth I suffered such immeasurable lows.

For starters, I wanted her to be a boy. Why? So that I could control and manipulate her life. But I couldn't control her at all. She cried all the time and I just didn't have the ability to stop her, so I ignored her. Or tried to.

Perhaps I was naïve and my expectations of motherhood were unrealistic. I knew it wouldn't be easy, but I really thought it would be achievable. I found it impossible.

Having a child is supposed to be a happy and wonderful experience. No, it was excruciatingly painful and the product at the end of it took control of my existence. According to the ridiculous letter that my doctor sent to

Social Services, I began to catastrophise as I fixated on the actual event of giving birth rather than the beautiful baby to which I had given birth. I was informed that catastrophising magnifies postnatal depression. I didn't go back to any more therapy sessions.

I turned my attention to my manuscript and I blanked Miriam from my thoughts. I made sure she was clean and fed, but she was never really a part of my life. I couldn't look after a new baby, so I spent most of my time ignoring her. The only energy I could muster was for writing my manuscript. I couldn't sleep at night without dreaming ridiculous dreams that just exhausted me. And during the day everything irritated me. The only way I could shut out the world was to write, write, write.

And, what was it that kept me going? The thought that when the manuscript was finally finished, I would take my own life and I would no longer be a burden to anyone, ever again. You would read my manuscript and you would understand how I felt.

I couldn't let my father see me like this; he would have quickly realised that something was immeasurably wrong, so I lied: I told you that he wouldn't visit me. With you, Anita, I made such an effort; please don't feel you missed the signs. I am an expert in my use of smoke-screens in life as well as in fiction. Forgive me.

Silva had affairs; so have I. Silva hated the opposite sex; he used them for his own ends just as I have done with men. I suppose he loved his wife, but even in that relationship she yielded to his domineering character. Anita, I have never loved a man in my life; I am, and always have been, self-obsessed. I have used the male race, since childhood, for my own superficial gratification. And it backfired.

And what about you? Who might you be in the manuscript? Did you think you were Kim, the best friend to our wronged Mary? How about Tania - of course, that is an anagram of Anita. But are you perfect? It would seem that perhaps my father thinks so. Oh, I have known about your affair for some time now. I should have realised that even you would eventually succumb to the potent magnetism that is my father. I feel that the most obvious

188

choice for you in the manuscript would be Lisa; and how contrived have I been again!

Many years ago on one of our fun filled singleton alcohol induced tête-à-têtes you told me about your second name. I believe it was your eighteenth birthday bash. At the end of the evening, I seem to recall that for once you were the one who had drunk too much, and why not on such a special occasion? In the morning you could not remember anything. But I could and did. This was the easiest anagram of all: Isla becomes Lisa. Simple.

Oh I was definitely Silva; the main character of my own novel. Self-obsession and egotism ruling my life as always. In fact, I don't think that my father was even in the manuscript unless, of course, he was Mary, manipulated by her father whereas in reality it has been the other way round. My father has been manipulated by his daughter. You see there is something else that I remember that no one else does because there is no one else alive to remember it. Crucially, it was Silva who was responsible for his wife's death; he was the one who insisted on having children. Crucially, I was the one responsible for my mother's death. My father didn't kill my mother - I did. Silva deserved to die; I deserve to die. Please allow me to explain.

My parents had been arguing yet again and mother grabbed hold of me telling me that she was not leaving me there with that maniac. I had been playing a game and I didn't want to go with her; I hadn't finished my game. Throughout my childhood, I had become accustomed to their constant bickering and I shut it off and focused on my own world.

Well, mum drove us off towards town and being prone to infantile petulance I decided to hit her on the head with the book I had on my lap. She lost concentration and the rest, as they say, is history. She died; I survived. I should have died. I never told anyone, thinking that even as a child I would be incarcerated for ever and the prison key would be thrown away. I blamed her for leaving me.

Do the following words strike a chord?

'I did not lose her. She left me. She allowed death to

189

take her into its welcoming arms. She wanted me
to love our child, the monster that had forced her
to leave me.'

Substitute 'our child' for 'my father' and you have my
life, my real life, inextricably intertwined with my
fictional life.

I could never look my father in the face again. He
didn't reject me; I rejected him. I have lived with that
guilt every single day of my life. My remorse has poisoned
my life and has become, in the words of Iris Murdoch 'a
fruitless mental torment' with which I can no longer live.
Ultimately, my feelings of guilt and grief were burdened
by failure: failure to admit the truth; failure to share with
anyone my innermost feelings; and failure to accept
anyone into my life.

If you love my father, Anita, - and I believe you do -
stay with him and together the two of you can nurture
Miriam, the wished-for child, far more than I could ever
have done. I cannot think of two people who are more
suited to cherish her.

'Being forced to live with an abusive parent is a life
sentence no child should ever have to endure; that
is poverty of the most heinous type.'

Sound familiar?
Take care of Miriam but also take care of every single
child in your career and ultimately in your care. All of
them have the right to a future where they can blossom.

With undying love,

Myra

P.S. Thank you for being so kind in your support of my
writing, but let's be honest - it was crap!

And so the final chapter of Myra's book of life is closed but not
forgotten.

The Chapters in Anita's Book of Life
(as yet to be completed)

Reality

Chapter One

Thinking about the Past:
Trying to Establish the Motivation

Myra Vilas folded over the navy waist band, raising the length of her school uniform skirt from just brushing the knee to about ten centimetres above the knee: a length that was definitely against school rules. She minced up and down the playground swaying her bottom from side to side and then stopped directly in front of me, twirled around like a fashion model before pausing and posing seductively. One hand was placed deliberately behind her head; the other alluringly on her hip. She experimented with various static poses before stopping and blowing me a kiss. Then she looked me in the eye and asked, "What d'you think?"

Anita Mann, quiet and unassuming Anita Mann, the classroom mouse, had been selected from among the crowd of potential soul mates to be the sounding board for this enigmatic new class mate. The confident Myra Vilas seemed to have left her childhood behind and was rapidly entering the world of adolescence and, for some unknown reason, wanted to take me with her.

A wolf whistle, clearly aimed in her direction, could be heard from behind.

Her reaction was immediate. She spun round, spitting venom, "I wasn't asking your opinion, dickhead."

The recipient of her abuse shrugged his shoulders, unperturbed, and walked nonchalantly past, "Please yourself." I would have wanted the ground to open up and swallow me whole, yet he did not appear to be at all disturbed by her angry dismissal.

She turned back to me, winked and stated quite categorically as if it were a well known fact, "Boys are idiots." I was hooked and thus the corporate and rather unusual friendship had begun at the tender age of eleven: the first day of secondary school. It was a friendship that stood the test of time.

Why had she picked me out from all the other girls? What did she see in me that was different and worth getting to know? We had not gone to the same primary school, but from that moment on we always sat together in lessons, except when split up from each other by the teachers for chatting and giggling too much in class. We spent every break-time and lunchtime together.

On one occasion, my form tutor asked me to stay behind after tutor time and warned me that she considered Myra to be a bad influence on me and surely I could make friends with someone more suitable. She believed that no good could come of our relationship and I should not get myself into trouble just to live up to my friend's expectations.

When Myra enquired as to why our tutor had asked to see me, I felt too scared to tell her the truth, wondering what her reaction would be. I told her that the tutor had wanted to talk to me about my French teacher's concerns that I was falling behind in class. This wasn't totally untrue as I had been finding the subject very difficult, but it was not why the tutor had wished to speak to me. I was fearful that Myra would see through me; I was not as adept as she was at concocting stories, but she just said that the woman was a silly cow who should mind her own business. To be perfectly honest, my academic progress was my tutor's business but I didn't argue.

I know that some of our classmates saw me as Myra's puppet, but I did not feel that way. There were times when she needed me just as much as I needed her.

We walked home together every day and always reached my house first. It was not for many years that I discovered where she actually lived. I am glad that I had not learned of her address during our early time together. When I asked her where she lived, she always lightly dismissed the question with a nonchalant, "Oh, down the road a bit further." Had I known that she resided in the 'posh' end of town, I would have been embarrassed by my small house in comparison with the mansion in which she lived. Myra Vilas, however, was never judgemental; she accepted me for who I was and contrary to my form tutor's opinion, did not try to change me.

She was, without doubt, the more outspoken of the two of us. She knew more than I did. Everything she put her hand to seemed to come naturally to her. She didn't have to work at anything: she was good at sport; she was academic; she was good at art and craft. Friendships would come and go but she always came back to me. She made me feel confident when I was with her. I felt protected. Sometimes, especially if I was feeling low, she would put her arm around my shoulders, being so much taller than I was, and whisper, "You'll be fine. You are who you are. People are nasty because they are jealous of you and would like to be you." She would squeeze me tightly; there would be a brief moment when she would look at me with those intense eyes before suddenly letting go and charging off, "Race you to the next lamppost." She could have beaten me every time but sometimes I am sure that she let me win. I never ever truly understood why she had picked me to be her bosom friend and I never will, but I have no regrets.

j

Reality

Chapter Two

Thinking about the Future: Fulfilling Myra's Vision

The interview was nearing its end and, although still feeling on edge, I was relatively happy that I had provided full and competent answers which showed me to be suitably qualified, capable and ready for this post of responsibility within the school. I had prepared well and, thus far, none of the questions appeared to have the purpose of catching me off guard or ensnaring me in a web of educational jargon of which some of the members of the leadership team seemed so fond.

I did, however, have some concerns about certain key players on the interview panel sitting in judgement before me. Those five individuals held my future in their hands. Each one of them had the power to extinguish my hopes for promotion; certain individuals undoubtedly held more influence than others and their judgement would be more pivotal in the final decision. I searched for a friendly face. I would certainly not find friendliness in the face of Mr Donald Strictland.

Mr Donald Strictland, the present Head of Department, who was about to retire, was totally and utterly in favour of setting in all years across the whole of the English Department's timetable. He had always insisted on having the top sets himself, with a self-righteous belief that no one else possessed the aptitude to teach the students at the higher end of the ability range. He considered that he had worked hard to get to the position where he could select which classes he taught; he certainly did not believe that Miss Anita Mann was able to take on the role of top set teacher, let alone Head of Department. I had not expected him to be on the panel; surely after he retired he would no longer have any influence in the school and should enjoy the years of luxury ahead? Department Heads were not usually present at the interview for their successor. He had clearly persuaded the Head Teacher that his input was vital. Actually, I would not be in the least bit surprised if he applied to become a governor after his pending retirement. I didn't think that he had ever taught anywhere else and even now was probably reluctant to let go of his post: once a teacher, always a teacher.

Donald Strictland and Mr Stuart Spence, the Head Teacher, had been close friends for many years. Although I had realised that Mr Spence would be on the panel, I had not bargained for the influence of his long term golfing and drinking companion.

The third member of the panel was a parent governor whose son I had taught during the previous two academic years. The son had been successful in English, achieving the top grade in both English Language GCSE and English Literature GCSE. He had enjoyed my style of teaching and his mother had stated at a number of parents' evenings that he adored me and credited me with his improvement in the subject. I was as sure as I could be under the circumstances that Mrs Warrington truly understood and was in full agreement with the direction in which I was trying to take my teaching and that of the department regarding my firm desire to introduce mixed ability teaching in English.

The teaching representative of the governing body was John Coburn. He was a scientist who often had semi-humorous discussions with me; frequently teasing me by saying that English could be taught by anyone and how science, on the other hand, took skill and formed the backbone of education. "Without science the world would be adrift; lost on a sea of mediocrity." I had to admit that, for a scientist, he possessed a poetic turn of phrase. However, beneath the humour was a man who loved his subject, loved his job, loved the students and always wanted what was best for them – every single one of them. He believed that the teaching profession was a true vocation and he was always willing to listen to new ideas even if they appeared to contradict his own.

By my calculations, this meant in theory that there was a fifty-fifty split in support of me. However, I was still worried about the strength of Mrs Warrington and John Coburn's opinion in the face of the potency of Mr Strictland and Mr Spence. I believed that the casting vote would belong to the Deputy Head and no one really knew what he felt. Sometimes he appeared to be a person who would just go with the flow, not wanting to upset the status quo. Yet, on other occasions he would seemingly play devil's advocate and no one was quite sure of his true allegiance in certain school matters. He held his cards close to his chest; he could be extremely cautious in his dealings with people and I wondered about his sense of loyalty to individuals. He was not someone I would trust with my innermost secrets.

Mr Spence informed me that there was just one final question from them remaining and then I would have the opportunity to ask anything that I felt to be imperative. The final questioner was Mr Strictland and I knew that this was going to be crucial.

His snake eyes bore into me. "You have, of course, studied all the data from recent years, Miss Mann, and as already stated, there has been an unfortunate trend of downward descent with regard to the English Language and English Literature examination results."

I could not help but wonder what other type of descent was possible, and was mildly surprised that Mr Strictland should succumb to tautology, presumably inadvertently, in his question. I considered it wise to make no comment but waited for the actual question to be given.

"How would you set about reversing this trend if you were to be Head of Department?"

I took a deep breath and plunged in: "At the present time all English classes are banded according to ability. I have to say that I believe that there is an element of elitism and unfairness in this approach."

'The whole system was totally and utterly unfair.'

I paused to see the disapproving eyes bearing down upon me. However, I continued regardless. "It may be argued that the system of setting groups favours the more able but I personally feel that there are very few, if any arguments, where this system might benefit the less able and it is in this area that the school's results in English need to be radically addressed. The results for the higher banded students also need to be reviewed, as although they are commendable to a certain degree, they cannot be described as consistent. All students, not just a minority, should be given the chance to achieve their full potential and become the best that they possibly can." *'By no means were the majority of young citizens afforded the opportunity to reach their full potential.'*

"In theory there should be fluidity between the ability bands or sets. In reality this has not happened and unless the different groups are studying the same text in literature, for example, the free movement between these sets is not actually a viable option. How can a child who has been studying George Orwell's *Animal Farm* suddenly be expected to be successful in a class that has been studying Harper Lee's *To Kill a Mocking Bird* for months beforehand? The setting is based on testing at the age of eleven and is rarely, if ever, reviewed after that time." *'It clearly favoured able boys at the age of twelve, with no regard for their growing maturity or intellectual development beyond that age. . . The result of the Elevation Examination was binding and irreversible.'*

"During the past two years, there has been some innovation with regard to the gender gap and the department has employed the system of having a separate top set for girls and another for boys. This has not made any noticeable difference to the examination results and further underpins the autocratic belief, inappropriate to the study of English with its propensity for diversity, that children should be separated by gender. We should return to mixed gender classes and mixed ability classes." *'It clearly did not favour girls in any way whatsoever.'*

Donald Strictland was starting to go red around the gills and seemed about to bluster in sheer disgust, when Mrs Warrington intervened quietly but effectively. "Could you please explain the advantages you perceive in teaching mixed ability English classes, Miss Mann?"

"Yes, of course. Recent research has shown that setting students tends to be for the benefit of teachers rather than the students themselves. The most important aspects of this establishment are the welfare of the students and their education.

Mixed ability grouping has a positive effect on the attitude and self-esteem of the students; they do not feel labelled or confined by an arbitrary consideration of their innate ability. Regardless of their ability levels allocating students to particular sets reinforces divisions of class and gender. By allowing high ability students to work with lower ability students, the diversity of skills can be redistributed to the benefit of all."

Mrs Warrington smiled, thanked me and said that she felt these ideas were very interesting. I was not surprised, however, when Mr Strictland did not give in so easily: a terrier with a tasty bone that he was not prepared to release without a fight. "Let us say, for the sake of argument, that we promote you to the pending vacancy for which we are at present interviewing, the Head of the English Department, but the corporate decision is to maintain setting within the department. How are you going to be an effective Head of Department when it is blatantly obvious that you do not agree with that decision?"

"Mixed ability practices can be fully utilised in the setted group to the benefit of all concerned. I am sure that you agree, Mr Strictland, that even when a group is in a specific ability band the need for differentiation is paramount. In recent years, our top sets have achieved a range of grades; perhaps, in hindsight, they should have received the benefit of a variety of approaches to suit their learning styles more appropriately. *All* students *'have a right to a future where they can blossom.'* I am more than happy to be involved in training with regard to employing effective differentiation techniques, not only for teachers in the English Department but in other departments across the school as well."

"Well said!" The resonant voice of John Coburn filled the room. "We would appreciate that in the science department."

Mr Strictland had been silenced: for now.

Mr Spence clearly felt that this discussion had taken its full course and thanked me for my contribution. He asked if I had any further questions, but I replied that I was more than happy and thanked them for giving me the opportunity to put forward my ideas. Mr Spence asked his personal secretary, who had been taking notes throughout, to take me back to the staffroom to wait with the other candidates.

I stood up, rather shakily if I am honest, but as I started to leave the room, Mr Strictland called me back, "Just one more thing, Miss Mann. You referred to research in your responses. Can you name *just one* influential educationalist who advocates mixed ability?" Clearly an intended fatal blow.

Myra's youthful words came to me. "You'll be fine. You are who you are. People are nasty because they are jealous of you and would like to be you."

I handed him a sheet of paper that I had kept in reserve in my bag for just such a moment. "Oh yes, of course, Mr Strictland. Do take this typed list of names and their specific areas of research within this field. I am sure you will find it interesting." I smiled, turned and left the room.

The Waiting Game

Three tense prospective Heads of Department sat seemingly together, yet disparate, in the staffroom. All of us waiting for the interview panel to decide which one of us, if indeed any, should be given the chance to take the English Department forward. It was a false and very awkward situation.

The bell indicating the end of the school day had gone just under an hour before. We all had preparatory work to be getting on with in our classrooms for the next day but not one of us was willing to leave the staffroom just in case the Head Teacher's personal assistant should return and call one of our names. This would indicate that the person in question should return to the Head Teacher's study and hopefully be offered the desired post.

I wished that I had brought a book to read. However, I knew that even if I had, I would not have been able to concentrate on it. It may have stopped me picking at the dry skin around my finger nails, but nothing more.

My misgivings rose to the surface and I started to agonise that I had gone too far in the interview. What was I thinking to label the system on which the English Department had relied for years as a form of elitism? Why had I criticised the examination results of the present incumbent, who just happened to be a good friend to the Head Teacher? Had I totally misread the situation? Why had I blundered on regardless of the cold response? I convinced myself that the job would certainly not be offered to me.

I looked fleetingly at my two colleagues, sitting across the table from me: both expressionless. Any inner turmoil either of them possessed was not in evidence outwardly. Had they been so impulsive? I doubted it. And what of them? What chance did they have of success? The situation was too precarious; this whole procedure was a sinister form of torture.

David Sheerman was a confident, if somewhat cocky individual verging on narcissistic. There was no doubting his ability as a teacher; he seemed to have a natural flair for the job. I saw him as my main rival.

The other candidate was Mrs Dickenson, a lovely lady, but she lacked fire. She was dependable; most students got on well with her. But there was no charisma, no 'oomph' as I liked to call what I perceived to be the vitality and magnetism that made a good teacher a great teacher. But was charisma a necessary prerequisite for Head of Department in a school that itself seemed to have lost its own 'oomph'? Perhaps it was the Head Teacher who should be the one who was about to retire, not just the Head of the English Department. My thoughts all jumbled together in a frenzy of uncertainty. What a mess! How I wished this would come to an end.

My thoughts were suddenly interrupted as my two 'rivals' shuffled uncomfortably, straightened out their clothing and sat upright in anticipation. Who would be the first to follow the Head Teacher's personal secretary into the Head Teacher's study? The lion's den awaited.

"Miss Mann." Mr Spence's secretary had entered the room and was calling my name. "Would you please accompany me to the Head Teacher's study?"

My immediate thought was that I had definitely gone too far and I was going to be given the sack, or at the very least be given a strong reprimand for my lack of respect towards my senior colleagues.

Like an automaton, I followed the personal secretary down the short corridor to the study. I had never noticed before how much she wiggled her bottom as she minced along in front of me.

I entered the room in complete trepidation. Mr Spence strode towards me with his hand held out, "Miss Mann, we would like to formally offer you the post of Head of the English Department. I have to ask you at this point whether you would be willing to accept."

I paused. Was this really happening? I looked at the faces of the other interview panel members around me: John Coburn with an "I told you so" expression; Mrs Warrington looking like a proud parent; and the Deputy Head nodding his head knowingly. Mr Strictland was nowhere to be seen and the paper, on which I had typed the names of various educationalists, lay scrunched up on the floor. At least my students managed to find the wastepaper basket when they screwed up their clandestine notes at the end of my lessons.

"Miss Mann?"

"Oh sorry, yes, I will accept. Thank you. Thank you so much for giving me this chance to prove myself. I won't let you down."

"Too damned right you won't. Staff training on differentiation from you next week. No elitism from now on." At which point John Coburn burst into laughter.

A more comforting and motherly voice ensued as Mrs Warrington added, "No, we know that you won't let us down."

"Suffice it to say, Miss Mann, that everyone in this room was in full agreement that you were the right person for the post. Young blood. Innovative ideas". *'Once again, congratulations on your success. You are now in charge. Welcome on board, you are the new Head of Government and Social Communication of Lithport. I look forward to us working together.'*

I grinned what must have been a ridiculous grin. I certainly did not believe that everyone was in full agreement that I was the right person for the job, but it really did not matter: the job was mine. *'This may not have been the right time to start indicating how she would embark upon enforcing her new powers, but she ventured her ideas anyway.'* "Yes sir. I would like to start by taking a fresh look at the setting system we have in place in the department if you don't mind." *'Lisa smiled, "Yes, sir. And I would like to start by stopping any movement of young girls from this fine township to other township training facilities".'*

Mr Spence continued as if nothing had been said. "Go home and have a well deserved glass of wine and we will talk things through next week. I look forward to working with you in your new role. If you will excuse me, I now need to speak with our other two candidates." He exited the room to personally enquire as to whether either David Sheerman or Mrs Dickenson required a debrief.

After hugs and words of congratulations, I left the building down a corridor and out of the side exit, thus avoiding the need to walk through the staffroom. I did not want to face David Sheerman or Mrs Dickenson just yet; that would have to come at a later date. I stepped confidently out in to the fresh air. My thoughts were unfettered. Not only was I ready for this new post, but I was also ready for the next steps in my private life.

I looked skyward, 'Myra, if you can hear me, I'm about to give Arthur one of the most important calls in my life. I miss him. I miss Miriam. So much. I am not going to lose them like I lost you. We are going to spend the rest of our lives together, of that you can be sure.'